D1197355

We Live and Die by Electricity

A Medical Mystery Novel

BY STAFFORD I. COHEN, M.D.

Paul Zoll MD; The Pioneer Whose Discoveries Prevent Sudden Death

Doctor, Stay by Me

We Live and Die by Electricity

We Live and Die
by Electricity

Stafford I. Cohen, M.D.

Copyright © 2021 by Stafford Cohen
All Rights Reserved

This is a work of fiction. Names, characters, places and incidents
either are the product of the author's imagination or are used
fictitiously. Any resemblance to actual persons, living or dead,
events, or locales is entirely coincidental.

Without limiting the rights under copyright reserved above,
no part of this publication may be reproduced,
stored in or introduced into a retrieval system, or transmitted,
in any form or by any means (electronic, mechanical,
photocopying, recording or otherwise), without the prior written
permission of the copyright owner.

First Edition
2021

Printed in the United States of America.

ISBN: 9798524688095

ACKNOWLEDGEMENTS:
I extend my gratitude to Bernard Mendillo,
who guided the first draft to the final publication of this book.
The book proof was reviewed by Deborah and Alfred. Their
recommendations were indispensable. I thank Judge David
Kopelman for his good advice regarding the jury trial.

For Adam, Nicole, Kenji and Mika.

Table of Contents

STAFFORD I. COHEN

Author's Note

We live and die by the electric currents of our hearts and brains. Life starts with the first heartbeat and life ends with the heart's last act or when the brain sends its last signal to gasp.

Life is an unsolved mystery that is no greater than the mystery of self-generated electrical signals that originate in cells within the life-sustaining centers of the heart and brain.

Life is reliant on these citadels and they in turn depend on each other. The heart and brain produce a sequence of orderly electrical signals that travel over their electrical grids. For the heart, an alteration in the normal sequence can cause an action that is absent or inadequate to circulate oxygen and nutrients throughout the body. Life ends if the spark that starts the sequence is extinguished.

So too, the electrical currents of the brain race through a complex network of billions of interconnected nerves that regulate involuntary activity, such as breathing. The normal electric traffic within the brain can be radically transformed into an epileptic seizure.

Man-made, electricity-emitting devices are used to treat deranged electrical patterns that cause life-threatening and near-life-ending heart action. Other creations are used to modify some neurological diseases and emotional disorders. These are inventions that harness electricity to reduce the adverse impact of pathological heart and brain networks.

Our lives are in a normal steady state when self-generated electricity from the heart and brain's dynamos are optimally organized. We die when those internal patterns are chaotic or

3

totally cease. Initial heart death is followed within minutes by brain death. Initial brain death is followed within minutes by heart death. Each organ is responsible for maintaining life-sustaining oxygen. Both organs and the entire body die without it.

We also suffer random electrical deaths when Nature's bolts of lightning strike someone. Although we have manufactured and tamed electricity for our benefit, when man-made high-voltage electricity flowing through our neighborhood grid is accidentally mishandled, it can kill. By judicial and penal-system statute, we have intentionally used high voltage to execute death-row convicts. Yes, intentional electrical death.

Just as life can be extended by man-made, electricity-emitting devices when guided by a noble person with a noble mission, so, too, life can be abruptly ended by man-made, electricity-emitting devices if guided by a sinister person on a destructive mission.

We Live and Die By Electricity.

Stafford I. Cohen, M.D.
Newton, Massachusetts

Chapter 1

It's a place that's teaming with humanity; a place where a member could drop dead and nobody would notice; and a place where few would care. At Manhattan's 312 East 86th Street, a lobby mailbox was full; its contents hadn't been collected for weeks. So the mailman left a notice dated April 2, 1976. It read: "Owner, pick up additional mail at the East 87th Street, Manhattan Post Office."

When neighboring condominium occupants strolled back and forth along the twelfth-floor corridors for exercise or to attend to their daily needs in the building, they complained of a bad odor emanating from suite 1214. The sole elderly resident, Joseph "Rocco" Vitale, was seldom seen. He hadn't been spotted by anyone for about a month—not even by the doormen who stood guard at this highly prioritized secure building.

Mike, the superintendent, was called. He, in turn, phoned Rocco several times. There was no answer, so Mike contacted Joseph Cornado, whom Rocco had listed as his "in case of emergency" contact.

Later that day, Mike and Cornado went to suite 1214. Mike knocked on the door and waited. No answer. Joe Cornado—well dressed, balding, pointed chin and stooped over—put his ear against the door. He listened for a full minute then said

"My hearing's no good. Do you hear anything?"

"Nope—nothing."

Then, squat and muscular Mike pounded the sturdy paneled wooden door with his fist until his ruddy-complexioned face turned bright red. Again, there was no answer.

"The odor smells like rotten garbage."

Mike didn't answer. He simply unclipped a key ring from his belt, selected one and inserted it into the keyway.

"It's time to investigate. This master key should let us in."

He turned the inner cylinder twice. Once to disengage the latch bolt; twice to keep it disengaged. The door didn't open. Not with a shove. Not with a kick.

"Damn, it's dead bolted from the inside. The door frame is solid steel. We won't be able to pry it open; we'll need some heavy equipment. Let's get back to the lobby. You wait there while I go to my workshop for the heavy-duty stuff."

They returned armed with a sledge hammer, a thick extension cord, a yellow electric-light lantern and a large-bore drill that could cut through anything.

Mike drilled out the lock, destroyed the steel door frame above the lock, identified an inch-thick deadbolt, narrowed its diameter with the drill and broke it with a few hard blows to the door frame.

When they entered, Mike's forehead was beaded with sweat. He took a few deep breaths, sat down and muttered, "Toughest door I ever had to open."

"What did you say?"

"I said—that door was a bitch."

Joe knew the layout of the suite. He went to the kitchen.

"No garbage here."

He then went to the bedroom.

"Mike! Come quick. Rocco's dead in bed with only his pajama bottoms on. Look, he's all blown up. His flesh is decomposing and stinks to high heaven. Call the cops. There might have been foul play. They'll call the medical examiner."

Chapter 2

By instinct, the cops believed that suite 1214 was a certain crime scene. They cordoned off Rocco's end of the twelfth-floor corridor, sealed the apartment, posted a guard at the busted door entry and, when a search warrant was issued, against the objections of Joseph Cornado, they requested a homicide crime team led by senior detective Dan Shanahan.

Shanahan had photographs taken of the corridor, the entry, Rocco's body and every room and detail within the suite. Shanahan and his two underlings put on shoe coverings and plastic gloves and then slowly moved about, eyeballing each room. Under the brim of his felt hat, Shanahan's grey eyes darted hither and yon. With each move, his raincoat's unbuckled belt ends swayed to and fro.

Onc of Shanahan's subordinates, Anna, was the daughter of a retired detective; the other, John, was the son of a merchant. John was an ex-marine; *ex* because he was wounded while serving as a demolition expert in Vietnam.

Paul Pedonti, Rocco's primary doctor at Mercy Hospital, said in a brief statement that he was familiar with his patient's ill-health, but was unaware of any imminent life-threatening problem. So, the medical examiner exercised jurisdiction for an autopsy because the cause of death was unknown.

Rocco was a notorious gangster who had survived in a crime culture infested with many sworn enemies. Shanahan told his team, "Don't overlook anything. This guy was high-up in the Davio Family. He had a lot of enemies. One or more might have issued a contract on his life in retaliation for his being a hit man."

The twelfth-floor suite was not elegant, just the basic essentials. The master bedroom had an end table with a telephone and a framed picture of a dark-haired attractive woman with each arm on the far shoulder of a flanking young boy. There was a bureau with three drawers, a bookshelf with files, a desk and a television set. There was a medium-size closet with a wall safe hidden behind a fake electrical fuse box. A connecting common bathroom had a sink, cabinet, tub and a shower. It also served another bedroom with a similar layout, but without a wall safe.

The kitchen had an electric range, refrigerator-freezer combination, a microwave oven, wall cabinets, countertops and storage drawers; one was loaded with medication bottles and some medical apparatus that included a combination blood-pressure cuff and stethoscope.

The living room held a sofa, low coffee table and two upholstered chairs.

Each twelfth-floor suite had only one entrance. On the opposite side of the corridor from Rocco's entrance was a room to store cleaning supplies. Adjacent to that was a stairwell with entry doors on all floors except the basement, but were keyed to bar exit from the stairwell to any of the floors other than the lobby. Once a person had entered the stairwell, the only exit was at the lobby within sight of the security desk. No stranger could enter a residential floor from the emergency stairwell.

The building had no balconies. Detective Shanahan thought it odd that all of Rocco's windows were grated and locked. If someone were to enter through a twelfth-floor window, it would be an acrobatic feat. You can't be too careful, he surmised.

The apartment's ventilation grates were very small; too small for even a child to crawl through. To be certain that nothing had been sequestered out of sight, Shanahan unscrewed the grates while he directed Anna and John to examine the toilet tank after removing its top. The detectives tapped the walls and the floor hoping to find a removable panel. No luck. The wall safe would have to wait.

Nothing seemed to be out of order. There wasn't an obvious clue that raised a suspicion of an unnatural death. The time had come to interview Joseph Cornado and Superintendent Mike. They were the ones who discovered Rocco Vitale's rotting remains.

Chapter 3

Cornado agreed to meet the detectives at Rocco's suite. He had nothing to hide. Yes, he was Rocco's lawyer. Yes, he had defended Rocco on many occasions when his client verbally threatened or physically abused an enemy during territorial encroachments or gang wars. Yes, Rocco had many enemies. He had been in the business for years and years. He was in charge of almost every Davio operation at one time or another.

Shanahan silently filled in the blanks. Every operation meant prostitution, hijacking, drugs, gambling and fixing outcomes in politics, sports, licensing and zoning.

When asked how well he knew Rocco, Cornado answered, "Better than anyone else. He's had his tough moments. Professional criminals seldom threaten a rival. They threaten the rival's family. Rocco used to have a family until his house on Staten Island was invaded when he was on a business trip. There were signs of a struggle. His wife and their two children disappeared. His wife was found—but she'd been terribly tortured and died in the hospital. His kids were never heard from again—that was in 1936."

Shanahan asked, "Any other family?"

"No. He was an only child. Parents are deceased and he never mentioned anyone on his wife's side. I think she was raised in an orphanage without known parents or siblings."

"How did Rocco react to losing his family 40 years ago?"

Cornado explained that Rocco knew his wife, Jean, had been brutally murdered on Staten Island; and after a while believed that his children suffered the same fate, but did not know when

11

or where. Having no relatives, he had only to be cautious and protect himself. Rocco had a list of suspects. He retired from running Davio operations, became a loner and a "specialist" at the behest of the Davios. When some of the suspects on Rocco's list died under suspicious circumstances, Rocco became a person of interest or was directly accused of shooting, poisoning, suffocating, torching or stabbing a fellow traveler. The prosecutors never had solid evidence.

"I successfully defended Rocco time and time again. He never served a day."

"Thanks for your co-operation," said Shanahan. "By the way, did Rocco leave a will?"

"He did. A colleague of mine drew it up. When the time comes, Hugh Appleton will file it," Cornado said, and then smiled and left.

Shanahan told John and Anna to investigate the 40-year-old Staten Island murder of Jean Vitale. They nodded.

Into the apartment stepped Mike, the burly building superintendent. He retold the sequence of events that had transpired with the complaint about a bad odor, contacting Joseph Cornado, drilling the lock and the deadbolt and finding Rocco's body. It was consistent with his prior statement.

"How long have you been the superintendent here?" asked Detective Shanahan.

"About five years."

"How long has Rocco lived here?"

"Long before I was hired."

"Who owns the building and who does the hiring?"

Shanahan was pursuing a line of inquiry that was not obvious to Anna or John.

"The owner is the East Side Building Trust. Rocco met me in the small basement apartment set aside for the superintendent. He hired me. If there's a problem in the building, I report to him."

"Are you aware of any big problems with this building before or since you've been here?"

Mike appeared to be in deep thought before answering.

"Oh—I heard that there was an explosion. A bomb went off outside Rocco's door. Blew the damned thing to smithereens. The blast did a lot of structural damage to the corridor—a lot of smoke, lucky there wasn't a fire. A construction company put everything back in order."

"Do you know how the assailant got by the security guards?"

"I don't know, but I heard that my predecessor forgot to secure the basement door that leads to the dock in back of the building. That door was breached. The only way from there to the twelfth floor was the freight elevator or the staircase. The super always has the freight-elevator key."

With that said, Mike unhooked his ring laden with keys, searched among them and with a smile on his face and a sense of accomplishment, held one up for all to see.

"Earlier, I thought you said the stairway doors only permitted egress," Shanahan said. "No one could enter."

"That change was made after my predecessor was fired and I was hired."

"Do you know the name of your predecessor?"

"No and I don't care to know."

13

"Why not?"

"I heard he was a spy from the Sarno Syndicate."

Shanahan told Mike that the interview was almost over. Just a couple more questions.

"Do you know why all the windows in Rocco's place are grated? Its twelve stories from the ground. Even that's too high up for a fire-engine ladder to reach."

"I'm not sure. A few years ago there was a spectacular penthouse robbery of a socialite. A masked cat burglar bound her hands and feet, silenced her with a mouth gag and took her precious jewels. The villain gained entry through a window while dangling by a rope that was secured on the roof."

"I remember the case well," interrupted Shanahan.

Mike went on, "That's when Rocco had the window grates installed—even though we're in a fifteen-story building."

"Can you remember the name of the company that installed the grates?"

"Sure. It's Empire State Construction and Maintenance Company. They've been with us for a long time. When I called, they came right away and said they were very familiar with the building."

"You can't be too cautious," said Shanahan.

When the interview was over, Shanahan asked Anna and John to learn the identities of the owners of the East Side Building Trust, to make a tally of the Trust's holdings and to learn what they could about Empire State Construction and Maintenance.

Chapter 4

The Jean Vitale cold case file was a compilation of gruesome photo images of the deceased and of the crime scene, recordings of Rocco's monologues taken by a hidden microphone placed in Jean Vitale's hospital room, conversations in the hospital recorded by other microphones placed by the police and listening devices that were already in place at the request of hospital security. The file also contained many interviews between law enforcement and persons of interest, witnesses and suspects. Rocco was among them.

The 40-year-old unsolved Staten Island Homicide File on Jean Vitale revealed a horrible murder and circumstances that would be forever excruciating for Joseph "Rocco" Vitale. When Rocco returned from a business trip, his home on Staten Island was empty. Some rooms were in disarray. There was evidence of a struggle. He thought, "What in Hell went on here?" He checked the hospitals to learn if his wife or two children were in an Emergency Department or had been admitted. He called the police and reported them missing. He checked the local morgue for any recent entries of any of his family or unidentified persons. The police sent out a missing-persons bulletin with a group photo of Rocco's wife, two sons and their distinctive identifying marks. The wife had a ripped right earlobe when its decorative ring refused to yield to a revolving door. She also had a forty-degree angulated left index finger from a fracture sustained when learning to roller skate. The older son, Joseph, Jr., had a partial facial palsy from a difficult forceps birth delivery. When Junior's mouth twisted during a broad smile, it was a small price to pay for survival. The younger son by a year, William, had a fractured nose that healed at an angle as well as a scar on his left shoulder from broken glass when he tried to batter open a locked door.

After a few frantic days Rocco got a call that his wife was near death at Staten Island Community Hospital. He was told that Jean had been admitted as Jane Doe several days before in a semi-coma that quickly deteriorated into deep coma from dehydration and bacterial septic shock. On entry, she was just another unknown, barely alive denizen snatched from the gutter of a city street. Half her clothes and her body were burned from the lower chest down to her ankles; facial flesh had been eaten away by acid that destroyed any semblance of lips or nose. There were no eye balls—only sockets.

Late on the second day, a half-balding, very short, sneaker-footed hospital administrator came to search for her identity and insurance. He had studied a board with tacked-on missing-persons bulletins and, while at Jane Doe's bedside, noted the fractured left index finger. He connected that observation with an admission nursing note in the chart that commented on hearing Jane Doe mumble the word "vital," a word close enough to "Vitale." Then he had the staff remove the total facial bandages and found an acid-spared, ripped, right earlobe. The sight was so grotesque, he pleaded with them to quickly re-wrap the entire head and face, with the exception of an entry for a breathing tube attached to a mechanical ventilator. His task completed, Jane Doe reclaimed her proper name, Jean Vitale. The police were notified and Rocco was called.

"Near death."

"Near death" kept echoing in his head as he rushed to the hospital. A volunteer at the information desk directed him to a small intensive-care unit with only four rooms.

When asked, "Where's my wife, Jean Vitale?" a sleepy-eyed clerk pointed towards the nearest room and said, "The priest and police have seen her every day."

Rocco entered the room emotionally exhausted; he folded himself into a chair at the bedside. His wife's head and face were totally wrapped in white bandages; she was under white blankets that reached up to her chin. From under their edges, wires and tubes either stretched to bottles or plastic bags on poles or to machinery.

Rocco softly spoke her name; no answer. He increased the decibels and finally shouted, "Jean." There was no response. He whispered, "What did I expect? She's dying. I'll just talk to her. Maybe she can hear."

So he spoke to her about when they first met at a church social in Queens. How they courted at movies, dances, and at private speakeasy nightclubs. They went to the Street Festivals that honored patron saints and, finally, he spoke of how they were only 21 when they married. Rocco reminded Jean that she had overcome adversity. As an infant, she had lost her family, was raised in the Saint Margaret Orphanage in the Borough of Queens, New York, and was never adopted or placed in a foster home. At the age of sixteen she went out into the world and lived in a one-bedroom apartment in a rooming house near the orphanage. Her good training in social interactions as well as her education as a skilled bookkeeper at the orphanage helped secure a job and promotions during the years that followed.

17

Rocco spoke of his own youth, about being raised by his father in the Italian enclave in Queens. His mother died from consumption during his teens. His father was a counterman at a local bar and grill. Like his dad, Rocco was an only child. His first job was running errands for Vinnie, the owner of the bar. When Rocco's father died in a tussle with a robber, Vinnie made Rocco his personal courier, gave Rocco escalating responsibilities and promotions and paid him a fine wage. Rocco never forgot his father's mantra. "To survive in this world—be tough; never back down; always do what your boss tells you to do."

After the birth of Joseph, Jr., the couple wanted their kids to have something that they never had: a home in the country with land, fields, gardens, animals and, most important—space. The nearest affordable location towards that goal was a home on Staten Island; a place detached from the hectic pace of New York, a place that was underdeveloped, and a place accessible by the most famous ferry in the world. So they moved there. They had a home. They had land. They had space. They kept their jobs. If one or the other had to work late and couldn't return home, friends provided accommodations in the city.

After reviewing that past history embedded with love during happy days, Rocco asked, "Darling, do you remember?" and then he was lost in reverie.

Rocco, sitting in a chair with eyes closed seemed to be half asleep until startled by loud bells and a loudspeaker voice repeating "Code Blue ICU. Code Blue ICU." Then there was the sound of approaching feet. People running past his room's open door and his room's large inner windows with pulled-back curtains. Rocco heard barked commands of only a word or two. Finally the sleepy-eyed clerk entered and said, "Emergency," then she closed the window curtains and shut the door. She returned about 20 minutes later and said, "Mister Vitale, I'm sorry for the disturbance," and retreated without opening the curtains, but left the door wide open.

As Rocco's gaze followed her route back to her desk, a patient in a bed was wheeled by the open door towards the exit. The patient was totally covered with a white sheet. A clump of doctors trailed behind. Some stopped at the nursing station; others sat at a table and appeared to be writing. One guy got up, walked a short distance and spoke to the sleepy clerk by the door entrance. She immediately picked up the phone.

Rocco reflected on the scene surrounding the emergency. He thought out loud, "That's what happens in hospitals. That's where people die." Once again, "Near death. Near death," echoed in his head.

"They said my Jean is near death."

Rocco reached under the blanket and held Jean's hand to provide some comfort to her and him. It was a warm hand.

"Is that the way it is when someone's near death?" he must have wondered as he clasped her hand with both of his. Sensing that something else was wrong, Rocco pulled back the blanket. Indeed something was terribly wrong. The index finger on Jean's left hand was straight. With a ray of new hope, Rocco bellowed, "Everything is wrong here. Maybe Jean's still missing. Maybe she was never near death."

At that moment, the sleepy-eyed clerk and the half-balding, short, sneaker-footed administrator entered.

The aide spoke first. "Mister Vitale, we've made a big mistake. We apologize." She paused and said no more.

Rocco was stunned and asked, "What mistake?"

The administrator answered in a squeaky voice, "You are not sitting by your wife's side. This is a patient with severe head and facial trauma who was operated on for her injuries. The operations were successful; she is still under the influence of anesthesia. Your wife happened to be in this specially equipped brain-monitoring room. Your wife was moved from here to the next room just before our clerk came on duty and unfortunately wasn't told of the move."

Not fully grasping the meaning of the words he just heard, Rocco spoke in anger, "Oh, I see. You scared the life out of me. You called and said my wife was near death. When I rushed here and asked for Jean Vitale, you sent me to this room. Are you people crazy, incompetent or both? I can't stand it here. I'm leaving to keep searching for her."

The clerk wept and returned to her desk.

The squeaky voice repeated, "It was a big mistake. We apologize. We sent you to the wrong room. Your wife was in the next room. She just died. Both this head trauma patient and your wife looked alike with their bandages. It was an honest mistake. Forgive us. Please understand and forgive us."

"She just died? I was here. I was right here when she died. I tried to comfort her. I would have comforted her. You denied me. You denied me. I'm still here. Take me to her."

"The priest is on his way to see another patient. He will accompany you to our morgue. Father Bartholomew will take you there. We told the Missing Persons Bureau that she died.

They told us to follow our homicide protocol. Now, Mister Vitale, follow me. You can wait in an empty room until Father Bartholomew arrives to be with you."

"No. I see an empty chair by the clerk's desk. I'll wait there. I don't forgive you. I can't forgive you. I will never forgive you. We were together for sixteen years. I was right here. You prevented my being with her when she died. Because of you, I will never be at peace until the day I die. May you die alone and be unremembered."

Father Bartholomew solemnly greeted Rocco and guided him to the subterranean hospital morgue that was a large refrigerator with six separate compartments. There was adequate room for a corpse to be placed on a sliding platform and rolled in feet first. The priest had a slip of paper in his hand upon which was written: "Compartment #2. Jean Vitale. Homicide. Do not disturb, move or displace anything on her person!"

The priest unlatched the door and rolled out the platform until the fully bandaged head with its breathing tube and sheet-wrapped shoulders came into view.

"Let us pray together," said Bartholomew. "Repeat after me."

"Wait, I can't pray to the Lord until I know who I am praying for. I can't tell who this is."

"Have faith and trust. The paper in my hand says it's your wife."

"I've just been deceived about who's supposed to be my wife. Let's remove the bandages and look at her."

"I can't do that. The slip in my hand forbids disturbing anything."

21

"Then I can't pray until I have a sign it's Jean. Let's just lift the sheet and let me look at—look at but not touch—her left hand."

Bartholomew had kind eyes, thick gray hair, a white beard and a wrinkled wise face. He rolled out the platform all the way and turned his back to Rocco. "Quickly, do or don't do what you just suggested." A minute later they faced each other. "I hope you're satisfied—can we pray together?"

After they prayed, they returned to the patient ward. The staff prepared coffee for them and they talked. Bartholomew told Rocco that he was aware that the hospital staff had made a big mistake and had asked for forgiveness.

"Don't forget—they were concerned enough to identify your wife. They tried to get you here before she died. Have compassion. Be forgiving. Follow our Lord's example and teachings."

"Father, I'm a believer. The Lord gives life and takes life. But the Lord was preoccupied when my wife was tortured, burned, had her face destroyed by acid and blinded when it eroded her eyeballs and the sighting fluids poured out. She was left in the gutter, not to die, but to be discovered. Gutter-swill bacteria invaded her burned flesh. She was meant to die after being discovered. Her torture was meant to be my torture. Why else would she and my children be kidnapped? Why else would she be returned as she was?

"Father Bartholomew, how can I forgive? My heart's burning with pain made worse by the hospital staff. How can I forgive those that took my family? I know too well how broadly and deeply our justice system is corrupted. I can't hope that the system will find and convict those responsible or take solace that they will burn in Hell if they don't repent. They don't know what they have unleashed. I will spare nothing to get my revenge. Sorry, father, I can't forgive today; maybe some other day."

Rocco told Father Bartholomew that they would not meet again. He would leave Staten Island for a safe and secure location elsewhere.

With that, they parted.

Chapter 5

Shanahan wanted to know more about Rocco's poor health. The sanctity of the doctor–patient relationship would prevent Paul Pedonti from revealing any information without the permission of an active patient, or without the prior authorization of a dead patient. So an interview with Paul Pedonti was probably out of the question. If someone were to be charged with murder by the prosecution, Rocco's medical records could be subpoenaed by a judge at the request of the prosecution or the defense.

If Rocco had died from "natural causes" there would be no charges and no defendant. So, there was no way to take a deposition from Paul Pedonti. Hearing that gloomy pronouncement, Anna suddenly lit up. Her thin body stretched to its full height. Her blue eyes sparkled.

"I've got an idea. Joseph Cornado said that he defended Rocco many times. Maybe during one of those times there was need for medical testimony. Maybe there's a public record; a court transcript with information. John, let's check it out."

Shanahan agreed and added, "Remember, someone said: 'Genius—or, as I like to say, success—is one percent inspiration and ninety-nine percent perspiration.' Don't waste time. Get on it right away."

Within a few days, Anna and John found a trial record from 1970 where "Squint" Malone, one of the Davio Crime Syndicate members, was accused of threatening a prosecution witness in a murder trial. At a later date, the witness fell, or was pushed, out of a tenth-story window, a day before his date to testify.

Anna and John called a meeting with Shanahan to discuss their findings. Anna summarized the substance of the case. The prosecution issued a subpoena for Rocco to appear as a "Squint" character, or, more likely, a lack-of-character, witness.

Cornado didn't want Rocco to appear at the behest of the District Attorney's prosecutors. That's when Dr. Paul Pedonti appeared with a claim that Rocco was too ill and fragile to be cross examined.

As Anna was telling her story, Shanahan speculated that Pedonti was not only Rocco's doctor in 1970, he also must have been the doctor for many members of the Davio Mob. If Pedonti let Rocco testify, the mob would extract their pound of Pedonti's flesh. If he did not let Rocco testify, the lesser problem was the possibility that a New York State agency would exercise extraordinary oversight of his medical licensing requirements and billing practices. So Pedonti gave a deposition about Rocco's poor health to prevent him from being interrogated.

Anna's exposition struck at the crux of Rocco's health. "Pedonti testified that Rocco had complications of long standing diabetes that affected his kidneys, the heart and circulation of the legs. Rocco's heart had a bad valve and disease of the major artery that carries blood from the heart."

The judge in the "Squint" Malone case agreed that Rocco was too ill to testify.

Shanahan interjected, "The diabetes didn't affect his vision. They say he was a marksman."

John spoke up, "Wait, there's more. While on a trip to Italy in 1968, Rocco fainted and was hospitalized. He had a very slow heart rate. The doctors labeled the cause, 'heart block.' The heart rate was so slow, he needed a permanent pacemaker. According to Pedonti's testimony, the Italian doctors, with obvious national pride, placed a Sorin Pacemaker System that was manufactured in Italy."

"His body was so bloated, I didn't notice," said Shanahan.

"That's not all. When Rocco finally returned to America, Pedonti had to check the pacemaker but couldn't locate an interrogator. All pacemaker manufacturers supply hospitals and doctors with interrogators for their branded pacemaker models. Sorin had no suppliers or agents in the USA, so Pedonti had to apprise the Italian Consulate in Washington, DC, of the problem. Consulate officials in turn got in touch with personnel at Sorin Manufacturing in Italy. Sorin shipped an interrogator to the Consulate that was immediately forwarded to 'Joseph Vitale, c/o Paul Pedonti M.D.' with an enclosed bill for three hundred dollars."

John stood, drank a glass of water, stretched and resumed his story. "Rocco reluctantly had to buy the darn thing. He had to keep the programmer with him at all times in the event of a pacemaker malfunction. For his own safety, he was not to let it out of his sight."

Ann interjected, "What were those doctors in Italy thinking? They could have used any number of American-manufactured pacemakers."

John continued to have center stage. "The ironic part of the story occurred two years later. Pedonti got a call from the Italian Consulate that the Italian Ambassador to the United Nations had been admitted to New York Presbyterian Hospital with a heart problem. Something about the Ambassador's Sorin Pacemaker didn't seem right and the attending doctors wanted to check it. But the only known interrogator east of the Mississippi River was owned by Rocco. Could he help out? Rocco agreed with certain conditions. First, he would loan the interrogator to the doctors at Presbyterian for only two hours. Second, the Italian Consulate had to send a limo to transport him to and from the hospital. Third, he was to arrive at the hospital just prior to high noon, so that while the doctors checked the ambassador's pacemaker, the limo would then transport Rocco to Oscar's Sea Food Restaurant for lunch. Fourth, the Italian consulate had to pay all the bills including Rocco's lunch."

The detectives agreed that Rocco had the last laugh.

By this time the forensic pathologists should have some preliminary information about the cause of Rocco's death.

After learning about the pacemaker, Shanahan told Anne and John to go back to Rocco's condominium and locate the Sorin Interrogator and its User Guide if there was one.

Shanahan added, "I think I saw them in a kitchen drawer with his medicines and medical paraphernalia. The condo's still considered a crime scene. I'll notify the police guard to let you pass. Remember, don't disturb anything else."

Chapter 6

While sitting across the desk from grey-haired, bespectacled, pipe-smoking Mortimer Baker, Shanahan asked, "Is there any evidence of foul play?"

"Can't say for sure."

"Why not?"

"No evidence of trauma. Death occurred at least three weeks before discovery. Most any poison would no longer be detectable, but we're running the tests anyway."

The bowl of the forensic-pathologist's pipe glowed as he took a deep inspiratory draught then exhaled a volume of smoke adding to that already beclouding the air in the small office.

"Mort, you shouldn't smoke. Don't you know it's detrimental to your health?"

"We did a total body x-ray. We found important problems with the brain and the heart. Rocco had a few scars on his brain; small strokes that might have been silent or caused a change in behavior. The heart's enlarged. The main artery from the heart—the aorta—is calcified and enlarged. There's a transvenous cardiac pacemaker system. The generator is placed below the left collarbone; its electrode wire is properly positioned in the heart's right-sided main chamber. We know that it's emitting a regular electrical signal seventy times a minute. We still have to learn more about the generator."

"How do you do that?"

"I called a cardiac electrophysiologist named Peter Merlino from Bellevue who works with us on these cases. He told us to gently extract the generator with the attached electrode wire so

28

he could test the system. The x-ray identified the generator as a Sorin Brand Pacemaker. Merlino said he's trying to locate a compatible pacemaker interrogator and wants any past records of the pacemaker's history and periodic check-ups."

"My team is working on that. Is there anything else that's puzzling you about Rocco?"

"Yep. He was shot."

"Shot! Why didn't you say so?"

That accusatory remark startled Baker. He choked and coughed so hard that embers from the bowl of his pipe in hand spattered over the desk.

Baker regained his composure.

"Where and when was Rocco shot?" Shanahan demanded.

"His back was riddled with buckshot. I can't say when; must've been a long time ago."

Chapter 7

After a successful search and identification of the principal owners and holdings of the East Side Building Trust, the principals and permits of the Empire State Construction and Maintenance Company and the Sorin Pacemaker Interrogator along with its instruction manual, Anna and John reported back to home base at Shanahan's office.

They admired Dan Shanahan, who was their middle-aged mentor. He grew up in Red Hook, one of the roughest, toughest sections of Brooklyn. His father, John, was a detective at the New York Police Department's 76th Precinct. His mother, Terry, was a spiritually devout, elementary-parochial-school teacher. Dan's sister, Beatrice, entered into the service of the church as a nun.

Red Hook was bursting with the illicit activities of several competing crime families. Notorious gangsters like Joey Gallo and Al Capone were born or lived there. Murders were commonplace.

Dan's father became his role model. John Shanahan was calm in the midst of chaos, clear-thinking when others were muddled, soft spoken while others shouted or loudly cursed. John's thoughts and actions were organized while those of others were unhinged; and, most important, no offer would change the direction of his predetermined moral compass. Simply said, John was a righteous and virtuous man.

Dan followed in his father's footsteps.

His workday was like the title of Eugene O'Neill's play, *A Long Day's Journey into Night*. Dan slept little but never became emotionally or physically exhausted. On the contrary, he had an endless reserve of energy and a mind like an overwound watch spring that welcomed a challenge. Dan followed every lead and considered pursuing each a "success," even when most led nowhere. A dead end was an opportunity to investigate another clue.

Anna spoke first.

"Dan, there is a connection between the Real Estate Building Trust, and the Construction and Maintenance Company. Both are owned and managed by many of the same administrators and private shareholders. They either support or are known members of the Davio mob. Cornado is on both boards of directors. The Real Estate Company fully owns, partly owns, or manages dozens of properties. That's how they hide their dirty money.

"They even own a bank that arranges the mortgages and loans. Each residential and business property has an onsite manager that gets a rent-free apartment or office. That was the arrangement with Vitale; that's also the arrangement with Cornado's law office; that's even the arrangement with Paul Pedonti's medical office. Once Pedonti accepted that benefit, he was obliged to treat the mob and have his independent medical opinion in some matters be overridden by the dictates of the mob."

Anna stopped talking to lift a cup and sip the free coffee provided by the police precinct. She hoped to be praised by Shanahan for her report, and she was.

"Congratulations, that report's covered with ninety-nine percent perspiration. Now, what did you guys learn after searching through Vitale's place?"

It was John's turn to speak about the evidence that he and Anna gathered about Vitale's pacemaker and its placement in Italy.

"When we searched through the kitchen drawers, we found a battery-powered machine labeled 'Sorin Interrogator' with its model and serial number. There was also a multi-language operation manual. The bookshelf held a file labeled 'pacemaker.' There was a discharge summary from the Milan General Hospital and a surgeon's operation note. Both were written in Italian. We took some photographs of the Sorin Interrogator with its identifying numbers. We brought in a photocopy machine to reproduce the Sorin owner's manual and the pacemaker folder. Everything was left in place, just as it was."

John broke out into a smile and had a look of satisfaction as he placed a bulging folder of information into Shanahan's outstretched hand.

"Good work. I'll get the pacemaker information to Mortimer Baker's pathology office. We'll have to requisition the Sorin Interrogator for it to be taken from the crime scene after dusting it for fingerprints. The electrophysiologist, Merlino, from Bellevue, will need the programmer to test the generator and the electrode-lead system. We should have no trouble getting an interpreter to transcribe the reports from Italian to English."

Then Shanahan told Anna and John to gather background information on Dr. Pedonti; and told them he'd be the next person to be interviewed.

"It's been a while since his brief statement about Rocco's health."

Chapter 8

At another meeting at the police precinct, Anna and John presented certifiable data on Paul Pedonti. John summarized their findings on a list and handed it to Shanahan:

- He's the son of Mark Pedonti, a well-known physician in Washington, DC.
- Paul's mother, Mary, was a nurse. The couple met when Mark was in medical school.
- Paul is an only child. His early education was at highly regarded private, rather than public, schools.
- Paul went on to Johns Hopkins College and Medical School.
- Post-Graduate internship and residency years were at New York University's Bellevue Hospital.
- He then became a member of the Department of Internal Medicine at Mercy Hospital.
- During the doctor draft for the Vietnam War, Paul was classified as 4F. That designation was a rejection because of an unstated medical problem.
- The New York Board of Registration in Medicine has not cited him for any ethical or illegal behavior. He seems to be a solid citizen.

After Shanahan read John's summary, he asked, "Did you learn why Pedonti is mixed-up with the Davio gang?"

This time it was John who had paused to sip from his cup of police-precinct free coffee. When he finished, the answer was, "Not a clue."

"Well, I'll ask Doctor Pedonti to meet with us where we can have privacy. He'll probably refuse without a lawyer like Cornado at his side. But we'll see."

To Shanahan's surprise, Pedonti agreed, with the proviso that he host the meeting at the Grand Bella Restaurant, that he be given the full names of Shanahan, his associates along with everyone's official titles and that their conversation be "off the record" without recordings or note taking.

On the appointed day, the maître d', with a breast-pocket name tag marked "Henry," escorted the Shanahan troupe down a corridor of numbered, windowless-door entrances to small private dining rooms. Henry paused at number 16, opened the door and with a flourish, properly seated the guests by their inscribed name cards across the table from Paul Pedonti. Menus, fine china and solid silverware were in place. After proper introductions, Paul Pedonti rose with a buzzing instrument in one hand and an attached wand in the other. He moved around to the opposite side of the table and waved the wand near each guest before returning to his seat.

Pedonti was satisfied, "Gentlemen and lady, thank you for complying with my wish that you not bring your brief cases and recording devices. Before we proceed, let's order lunch."

He signaled the waiter by pressing a button on the table. The waiter entered. The guest menu had a gourmet selection of international cuisine; too many choices for a quick decision. When the guests finished their selections, the waiter turned to Pedonti.

"I'll have the usual."

After the waiter left, the business of the meeting began.

"Now detectives, how can I help you?"

Anna and John turned towards Shanahan, who asked, "Doctor Pedonti, how did you get involved with the Davio group?"

"That's a long story. I'll try to be brief. One morning, when I had just joined the faculty at Mercy, I was driving to work. When stopped at a red light, I heard a series of irregular loud popping sounds. Then two guys suddenly opened the front and back-passenger doors of my car. The guy at the front door struggled to get in. The other gorilla-like guy jumps into the back seat, waves a pistol and says, 'We were just pedestrians. We've been shot at. My buddy's been hit. Get to the nearest hospital as fast as you can.'

"I looked at the guy sitting next to me. Bright red blood was pouring from his mid-left leg onto the seat and floor. The traffic light was still red like the color of blood that's pumping from an artery, so I unbuckled my belt, pulled it loose, wound it around the victim's upper leg, slipped the end through the buckle and pulled it as tight as I could. I told the poor devil to keep pulling the belt as tight as he could.

"From the back seat, 'Move this damned car now. Get going as fast as you can. Forget about the traffic lights. Go!'

35

"The Metro Hospital was only about four blocks away, so I raced towards it, blowing my horn while navigating through cross-directional traffic. When we got to the emergency department, the guy in the back hops out, opens the door of his dazed buddy who was still clinging to the end of my belt strap, and says to me, 'Thanks. Take off. Say nothing. We owe you one.'

"I slowly turn my car towards the exit lane and watch through the rear and side-view mirrors. The brute had picked up his buddy with the dripping-blood-drenched pants and was walking toward the emergency-department entrance. He looks back to be sure that I was leaving and likely to remember my license-plate number."

Anna couldn't contain herself.

"What happened next?"

What happened next was a knock on the door and the wait help entered before Pedonti could respond.

All of the detectives' meals were elegant compared to their "standard fare." Pedonti's "usual lunch" consisted of garden salad, haddock with seasonal vegetables, mushrooms and a side dish of cheese. His beverage was a glass of milk. The wait help left immediately after properly placing the meals and asking the guests to select from a variety of warm rolls, butter, cheese and beverages.

Pedonti resumed his story.

"What happened next was listening to my radio while heading back home to change from my blood-stained clothes. The radio program was interrupted by a news flash.

" 'A security guard foiled an attempted robbery at Second Madison Mortgage and Loan Association. Gunfire was exchanged between the guard and a pair of robbers. The robbers sped off in a getaway car driven by their lookout. One was so badly wounded that he was dropped off in critical condition at the entrance to Metro Hospital.'

"I realized that I was a wanted man. I finally arrived home, called in sick, changed my clothes, scrubbed down the front vinyl car seat, threw out the blood-soaked floor mats and vowed that I would never ever again leave any of my car doors unlocked."

With a mouth half full of veal scaloppini, it was Shanahan's turn to interrupt: "Wow, another example of an unrewarded good deed. You're in a pickle. Who were these guys?"

"There were intermittent news reports about the robbery. The wounded guy survived. He was semi-conscious and in blood-loss shock when dropped on the ground near the emergency department entrance. During his recovery, he had no memory of anything and so-called witnesses could only remember seeing guns and hearing gunfire. The security guard sprang into action when an alarm was triggered by the cashier. The robbers, one with a gun in hand, ran towards the exit. No one could describe the getaway car. The guy with the gun was never found. The guard identified the wounded guy in a lineup. After a few years, I nearly forget about the entire affair."

Another knock preceded the re-entry of the waiter to clear the lunch dishes and to take orders for desert. Pedonti ordered a dish of mixed nuts. The detectives ordered spumoni, or crème brûlée, or chocolate cake and coffees like espresso, cappuccino and Arabica.

Alone, once again, John asked, "We still don't know how you became the physician to Vitale and his friends."

"I told you that it was a long story. We're almost there. I received notice that my medical office building was to undergo a total renovation and be unusable for six months. The management company would temporarily move the tenants to other buildings that had vacancies until the offices were ready to be re-occupied. I met with a management representative from the East Side Building Trust. He told me that I was first in line for a new location. I could choose among several in what might be called 'Doctors Row.' Imagine an office in an upscale neighborhood within a short walk to the hospital, whereas my current office was in a lower-middle-class neighborhood at a distance from Mercy Hospital. What an opportunity. I selected the best location. When I asked about the differential in the rent, I was told by the representative that upper management hoped that I would select that building because I could be installed permanently in the new office, rent-free, if I agreed to be the building's on-site manager. The current manager was to retire at the end of the month. The offer was too good to be true, so I accepted on the spot. I learned that once they do something for you, you're beholden to them forever. It's hard to refuse a patient that they refer. That's how I became the doctor to Rocco Vitale and the Davio family."

Pedonti glanced at his wrist watch,

"Sorry, I have to get back to the office. If you have further questions, we can meet at another time. Same conditions. Stay in touch."

Before leaving, the detectives thanked Pedonti for being such a generous and gracious host. Then Shanahan asked, "Do you know why you were picked for such special treatment by the real-estate company?"

"When I asked, 'Why did upper management pick me?' The representative answered, 'They owed you one.'"

Chapter 9

There was another meeting hosted by Pedonti at the same place with the same rules. Note taking and recordings were banned. During the first meeting, the detectives' questions were answered with apparent honesty. They learned a lot, but were unclear why Pedonti was cooperating or why he wasn't accompanied by a lawyer.

During the brief interval between meetings, the menu at the Grand Bella Restaurant had changed, so Pedonti's "usual" garden salad became an avocado salad and his main course became a filet mignon rather than fish.

When asked why he preferred dairy and beef which was believed by most health experts to be detrimental to the cardiovascular system, Dr. Pedonti answered, "I need a ketogenic diet to control my epilepsy. It started when I was a child. First there was a seizure during a high fever that the doctors believed to be an anomaly. Then intermittent seizures occurred that did not respond to medications. Finally when I was in high school, in desperation, a specialist suggested a ketogenic diet. It's simply high protein, high fat and low carbohydrate.

"In the very beginning, I had what's called a 'march.' An epileptic attack would start with involuntary shaking of my left hand. The shaking would progress up my arm to my shoulder then take over my entire body in what's termed a 'grand mal seizure.' I would pass out and when I regained consciousness, there was usually a fuzzy image of someone hovering over me. I had no immediate recall of events. Some attacks were more embarrassing than others, especially if I lost bladder control.

"The nurses at my elementary school and high school took good care of me. My school chums looked out for me. During my senior year they offered to take me anywhere when they were permitted to drive an automobile and I wasn't."

Anna abruptly stopped eating when Pedonti described his epilepsy. When he paused, she said with compassion, "What a tough scary deal, having to cope with unpredictable attacks."

"It was scary and dangerous. I could've fallen and cracked my skull open, drowned in the bathtub or collapsed in the middle of a thoroughfare. It was scary for my parents. I've always believed that worrying about me made them overprotective and was their reason not to have another child."

When John interjected that epilepsy could be caused by head trauma of the type that he'd often seen in Vietnam, Dr. Pedonti acknowledged that he'd wanted to go to Vietnam, but epilepsy disqualified him from serving in the military.

Dr. Pedonti then went on to give a primer on epilepsy. "The doctors couldn't figure out what caused my problem. The brain never rests. Its billions of cells generate constant currents of electricity routed along a vast interconnected electrical grid. Certain areas of the brain regulate emotion, speech, memory, breathing, heart rate and any number of other functions. Normalcy is when the electrical networks are regulated, that's when electrical signals flow uninterrupted, smoothly and in a proper progression. If an 'irritable' area on the surface or subsurface of the brain suddenly discharges a series of electrical signals that override what's normal and invade the interconnected 'wiring,' the result is a seizure. Medication or diets that change the environment or chemistry of the irritable focus either eliminates the unregulated electrical discharge or prevents it from invading other cellular pathways.

"The brain's electrical signals can be recorded on a skull-surface machine termed an 'electroencephalogram.' Epileptic-seizure activity can be recorded as well as other diagnostic patterns. Even brain death has a generic wave pattern when needed if it's not clear that a comatose or beyond-coma patient has a capacity to receive information or any future ability to respond.

"Fortunately, since I've been on the ketogenic diet and a little medicine, I've only had the start of an epileptic 'march' that stops below the elbow. Yet, you never know what might happen tomorrow."

"You've had to cope with a measure of insecurity with your health," said Shanahan. "We applaud your resiliency in dealing with it. Now, with your permission, let's get back to Rocco. We're sure that there was foul play. We know he had enemies and we have a couple of suspects in mind. Did he ever act like he was in danger?"

"He was suspicious of everyone. We had to schedule his appointments under an alias. He insisted on having the first appointment and leaving by a stairwell exit rather than through the waiting room entry. He behaved like he had enemies and was in danger."

"How's that?" asked John.

"When I first met him and took a baseline chest x-ray, he'd been hit with double 00 buckshot. I asked how that happened. Rocco told me it was an accident while pheasant hunting in the Pocono Mountains. I didn't believe him. When I was young, on the first day of the deer season, my friends joined the hunt; their ammo was double 00 buckshot. Pheasant hunters use a smaller size. Double 00 can kill a person if discharged from a 12-gauge gun by someone who's not an accurate shooter. In any event, shot pellets are made from lead, so I had to check Rocco on occasion for the unlikely possibility that he might have symptoms or signs of lead poisoning. Problems like anemia, renal failure or a change in mental status. The last would be difficult to determine because Rocco was volatile, ranging from anxious to calm to paranoid."

Anna asked, "Paranoid in what way?"

"He refused to have me place anything in the record about his roots, his parents, or his nuclear family, before or after they disappeared. While he was alive, I could not share any part of his record with anyone or any other doctor without his permission. He only gave permission to share information with his lawyer, Joseph Cornado."

"Do you have other patients like that?" asked Shanahan, hoping that other members of a crime syndicate might be exposed.

"No, not to that degree. Rocco wanted total secrecy. Some patients want information hidden from a former spouse, while dividing assets of an estate, litigation about liability in a death, or a division of business assets."

"Even though he was paranoid, did you have reason to believe that he was in danger?" asked Shanahan, while sipping an end-of-lunch liqueur.

"I thought so. He had intermittent irregularities of heart rhythm. Some were brief, others prolonged. My colleague,

Thomas Marks, a heart-rhythm specialist at Mercy who follows his pacemaker, warned that the arrhythmia, termed atrial fibrillation, might result in the formation of a heart-chamber blood clot that could lead to a stroke unless Rocco took blood thinners like warfarin. When Rocco heard the recommendation he got agitated, then asked, 'Isn't that a type of rat poison I've used to cause them to bleed to death? Those dying rats weren't a pretty picture.' After I told him that warfarin's use in humans is done with doses that are carefully adjusted by blood tests to prevent over dosing that might result in bleeding or under dosing that might result in blood clots, Rocco appeared to be in deep thought, then said, 'Can't risk it. I'd rather take my chances with a stroke than bleed to death from a stab wound, a bullet or a smashed head.' "

Dr. Pedonti glanced at his watch.

"That should wrap it up. This will be our last meeting—too risky for me to have another. The crime syndicates in this city are perpetually at war. When they're not in open conflict, they spy on each other. I'm glad we spoke. I'm tired of being told by the Davios who I must see in the office and what I must say as an expert witness. They have agents and even double agents. I learned that the on-site-manager I replaced didn't retire; he and the building's superintendent disappeared when an informer told the Davios that both were spying for the Carderelli Syndicate. In the fifth century B.C., the Chinese military strategist Sun Tsu developed a number of principles relating to the art of conducting a war. One of the most important was to 'know your enemy.' That required spying on enemies and infiltrating their ranks. There's no record of our meetings here. Henry took care of that. He believes that I saved his life during a medical crisis. He protects me. Good luck with your investigation. If you want to know more about Rocco's health don't ask me, contact Doctor Marks."

Chapter 10

The first stop for John and Anna was the courthouse to learn if Rocco's will was on file. They discovered that it was filed in Probate by Hugh Appleton. Rocco had no living relatives. He had extensive real-estate holdings as well as brokerage and bank accounts. His long-term lawyer, Joseph Cornado, and the New York City Archdiocese were the only beneficiaries of Rocco's estate. Cornado was to receive 99.5% and the archdiocese 00.5%. Cornado likely dictated the terms of the will to Appleton, who was an associate, because the person that draws up the will can't be a beneficiary—too great a temptation for an unethical lawyer to exert "undue influence" on a client. It's been known to happen. Some attorneys are rascals. John and Anna wondered if Cornado's large inheritance would be a motive for him to rush Rocco's death.

The next stop was to go back to the pathologist with Shanahan and learn if Mortimer Baker had any further information. Anna's new role would be to take charge of the meeting.

Anna Dixon was the daughter of a disgraced detective. An internal investigation turned up conclusive evidence that he was dealing drugs and shaking down some business owners in a protection racket. It started after bad investments led to debt— and ended with desperate measures and unethical criminal behavior that were hard to change. When discovered, detective Dixon voluntarily retired to keep his pension. The family was disgraced. Anna never forgave her father—and then went on to study criminology, join the force and vow to salvage the Dixon name.

Mortimer Baker clenched his ever-present pipe as it traveled from hand to mouth and back. Anna asked if he found any evidence of foul play.

"The toxicology tests were all negative. No indication of poisoning. The brain had signs of small non-compromising infarct scars from blood clots that originated in the heart and travelled to the brain. The dilated enlarged calcified aorta was primarily the result of syphilis. We call it 'luetic aortitis.' The calcified leaking aortic valve was a secondary effect and the slow heart rate was a third, long-delayed effect of syphilis. Thick calcium in the aortic valve ring invaded a critical adjacent electric pathway that prevented electrical signals that originated in one of the heart's natural pacemakers from reaching the main pumping chambers. Rocco was lucky that the usually unreliable, slow, secondary pacemakers took over. That's why Rocco needed an urgent artificial pacemaker."

Mortimer with pipe in hand moved the stem toward his mouth. He sealed his thick lips around the mouthpiece of the pipe stem and deeply inhaled. Then he paused.

"Someone must have treated his syphilis," said Anna.

Shanahan finally spoke. "Don't forget, Rocco was in charge of many Davio operations including drugs and prostitution. There must have been a number of sex workers willing to trade 'a consideration' for a favor from Rocco."

The long silence that followed was finally broken by Dr. Baker: "That was long ago. Even when treated, the 'wages of sin' are long lasting."

Anna resumed her questioning of Baker: "What did you learn about the pacemaker? Was the system intact?"

"Peter Merlino tested the system with the interrogator. The battery had plenty of juice and the wires were intact without fractures. The Sorin Generator was emitting electrical pulses at 70 beats a minute that were at an adequate voltage and duration. Rocco did not die from a pacemaker system failure, a massive stroke, poisoning, internal bleeding or trauma. I'm not sure why he died. But I found no evidence of foul play."

"Can you help us with a reason how he might have died?" asked Anna who was desperate for a clue to support her team's theory that an enemy or "friend" of Rocco had done him in.

"One possibility is that Rocco had a cardiac arrest from ventricular fibrillation. The main chambers don't contract and relax; the entire heart just wiggles from chaotic electrical activity. In that state, the main chambers can't pump blood. Rocco's pacemaker can't correct that problem. Ventricular fibrillation is a common cause of sudden death and it leaves no identifiable hallmark for me to discover at autopsy. That's why it's only a theoretical possibility. If ventricular fibrillation did occur, I'm sorry to say that it was caused by the invisible hand of the Lord rather than one of Rocco's enemies."

Baker paused and took another puff of his pipe, then asked not to be put in the middle between Shanahan's detective unit and Joseph Cornado who had made several inquiries that the body be released to the funeral home for cremation.

"My autopsy's finished. I can release the body now. I've saved a lot of tissue samples and can reassure the crematorium that I removed the pacemaker. You know, a pacemaker will explode if exposed to intense heat. More than one furnace has been unwittingly damaged by a pacemaker explosion.

48

Fortunately Vitale's pacemaker and leads are with Peter Merlino."

Shanahan asked for more time to complete his investigation. His wish was granted by Dr. Baker.

Mortimer Baker handed Anna the Sorin Programmer and owner's manual. She thanked him.

Anna asked Shanahan to call ahead for permission to have the guard let her and John enter Rocco's suite so they could return the interrogator and manual to their proper place.

Chapter 11

When John and Anna passed the police detail to enter Rocco Vitale's suite, they were surprised to find a couple of electricians in the apartment. The Davio hierarchy had anointed Joseph Cornado with the title of "onsite building manager," so he was given permission to live in Rocco's suite. Now he had two rent-free accommodations; one for his office and another that would soon be his residence, once Rocco's death investigation was finished. Cornado belatedly sent the electricians to fix the security camera that scanned the twelfth-floor corridor. It was mounted on the ceiling at the farthest end, a few feet from the entrance to Rocco's suite. About a month earlier, the guards who were at the security desk reported the failure to Rocco, the long-term building manager. Their custom was to write up a repair slip and place it in Rocco's in-house mail slot. The guards noticed that their slips were not being processed, so they phoned Rocco and left messages on his call machine that went unanswered. Cornado had a backlog of building repairs to tackle.

The electricians had a yellow logo on their blue work shirts: Empire State Construction and Maintenance Company.

John flashed his police badge then asked the older-appearing of the two—the one with white hair, a gray mustache and acne-scarred face, "What's the problem?"

"The camouflaged, security Seeing Eye outside the door failed."

"What was the cause?"

"Nothing much, just a blown fuse. It was easy to figure out because I installed the Seeing Eye."

"When was that?"

"Years ago, after a bomb exploded outside this suite. Mister Vitale insisted that we install security cameras throughout the building. It was a big job. He wouldn't let us tie 'his camera' into the main total security network. We had to electrify 'his camera' from his fuse box and run a separate line to the viewing room. In that way it would be harder to disable remotely. This is a big building with a complex system."

"Hmm, does the camera have a memory loop?" asked John.

"His does. Unlike all the others in this building, his is top of the line. It's really not a camera, but a tiny Seeing Eye. In the viewing room, it has a huge memory—seven days. At the time, no one in the industry made a better Seeing Eye and the other cameras in this building have either no memory, or a much shorter memory loop."

John asked, "What happens after seven days?"

"They replace the used tape with a new one, keep the used one for a while and then erase and recycle it."

John and Anna returned the Sorin programmer and the instruction manual. They then left the suite with the electricians. In doing so, they waved towards the area of the surveillance eye that had just been reactivated.

Until this moment, Anna had been a silent observer. Earlier in the day, she had questioned Mortimer Baker, so she let John interrogate the electricians.

"John you were brilliant. Let's contact Shanahan right away. We don't have a moment to lose."

When Shanahan arrived, the three of them needed information from the security guards.

The guards worked in pairs; their uniforms bore the yellow logos of the Empire State Construction and Maintenance Company. Both guards appeared to be structural descendants of gorillas, the largest primates that evolved alongside protohumans. Both had silver-gray hair protruding beneath the rim of their caps. They were in their late middle years and were armed.

John continued to assume the role of the lead investigator with Anna and Shanahan silent, but alert and taking mental notes of everything.

John Knight was proud to be in the moment leading an investigation. His resumé revealed that he was an only child who came from a small town in New Jersey. His parents owned a Mom and Pop hardware store. John's mother, Carrie, was posted at the cash register. John's father, Courtney, did everything else. When John was old enough to work without violating the child-labor laws, he stocked the shelves and posted the prices on each item. Hardware stores carry hundreds of items and brands. John had an excellent memory with recall of the exact place that the items were located and gradually learned their purpose. After the store was robbed on a cloudy night when thieves forced open a window, a perimeter alarm system and a security camera were installed. John was angry that his dad had suffered a large financial loss from the robbery, plus added expenses to protect his store from future criminals. That's when John got a shortwave radio to listen in on the police, ambulance and firefighter band widths. He memorized license plates of stolen cars and the facial features of mug shots on the "most wanted" bulletins displayed at the post office. His calls to the local police with "leads" led to several arrests.

After graduating from high school, John planned to enter the Police Academy but his number came up for Army induction for the Vietnam War. At boot camp, his placement test indicated that John had "nerves of steel," remained calm when others were prone to terror and had a very steady hand that would not disturb the hair trigger on a boobytrap. So John was trained as a demolition expert—to de-activate bombs and landmines. He performed his job admirably until the truck that transported him and his buddies was blown up by a landmine. John was lucky to survive his multiple injuries. After he recovered and was discharged, John matriculated to the Police Academy.

All that was behind him. Now, in the moment, John flashed his badge and spoke softly: "We're here to view the last security tape recording taken outside Mister Vitale's twelfth-floor apartment. Can you escort us to the viewing room? We also want access to your sign-in and sign-out logs that record the people who come into the building and leave. We need the names, times and dates."

The older-appearing guard said, "Pleased ta meet ya. I'm Crusher. Things have been quiet here. Nothing like a little excitement. Bruno, you stay at the desk, I'll show them the way."

Off they went down an indistinct corridor. Crusher stopped at an unmarked door, pulled out a card from his shirt pocket, silently mouthed what he read, made a fist and rapped at the door. Then, after what must have been a coded series of knocks, the door opened.

The room was small. A short, obese woman with blond-streaked black hair and purple-framed thick-lensed eyeglasses stood at the threshold almost blocking the view of three horizontal banks of black-and-white images on screens along one wall. There were twelve in total. Crusher introduced the visitors to "Sister" and left.

John flashed his police badge again. He asked that Sister get the last recording from Vitale's twelfth-floor camera on the day it failed. "We will start there and work backwards if necessary."

"Of course; so nice to have visitors. We work here on eight-hour shifts. It gets lonely sitting behind that desk watching screens for eight hours."

While Sister was methodically going through one of several file cabinets to get the film, John took mental notes of four telephones on Sister's desk. The desk had a built-in red button at the far left-hand corner, a poorly camouflaged built-in brown button on the far right-hand corner. As for the rest of the room, there was a half-open door to a lavatory and a small refrigerator. Sparse.

"Well, I finally got it," said Sister, as she positioned the reel into a viewer. "The film can't leave the premises and can't be copied—so don't ask. You came just in time. We planned to erase and recycle this film next week, but I can preserve it if you make a formal request. By the way, I work from 8:00 AM to 4:00 PM. I'm off duty in ninety minutes. That's' when my relief arrives. Another woman, my sister—only me and my sisters work here. You know, my sisters and I have much longer attention spans than men." She stopped, rolled her eyes and continued, "My name isn't Sister, it's Frances. My sisters and I resemble each other. Crusher can't remember who's who, so he calls each of us 'Sister.' Now busy yourselves with the tape and viewer. You have only an hour. If you don't finish, you can request that we preserve the film and make an appointment to return another day."

Sister delivered that speech without taking her eyes off the monitor screens.

John was at the viewer controls; Shanahan and Anna hunched over to see the screen as John fast-forwarded the reel to the end and slowly rewound the reel until someone came into view at Rocco's door. That *someone*, during continued reversal of the reel, walked backwards to the beginning of the corridor.

Shanahan spoke for the first time, "Great. Now have him advance in slow motion."

The *someone* had the appearance of a young man, average height, wearing a dark wind-breaker with some form of identity badge pinned to it, gray pants, and carrying a bulging briefcase by its handle in his right hand. He stopped at Vitale's door, placed the brief case on the marble floor, knocked, picked up the case and was let in. At that moment, the date and time code on the film read March 12, 1976. Sixty-two minutes later the film went blank before *someone* left the apartment.

John fast reversed the film to the beginning, motioned to Sister, handed her the reel and said, "Got a good look before the time was up. Preserve the film. Do not destroy it. Thanks for everything. Can we leave now?"

"Glad you got what you were looking for. Crusher will escort you out. I'll summon him."

Sister returned to her desk, continued to stare at the monitor screens as her left hand extended and depressed the red button once. Shortly thereafter, there was a sequence of knocks. Sister opened the door and the detectives left.

When they arrived at the lobby, John asked Crusher, "Did you collect the log books?" John added, "We want to review the one that includes the month of March, 1976."

"Come by tomorrow, I'll have it for you."

Chapter 12

The next day, the baton was passed to Anna. She was to be in charge. Crusher had his associate Andy Scarnici escort the trio of detectives to an office that bordered on the main lobby. Andy was short, about five-foot-five, broad shouldered, thick necked, greying hair, depressed right temple and drooping right upper eyelid. It was difficult to know if that eye had sight. The log book was at a corner of a long table. Anna sat at the head, John at her right side and Shanahan to her left. Andy Scarnici stood. The headings of the vertical columns were Date/Name/ Organization/Destination/ Entered/ Departed. Anna searched the Destination column until she came upon Vitale, twelfth-floor. To the left was the Date: March 12; Name: Owen Holden from Dr. Thomas Marks' office. Entered: 2:15 PM; Departed: 3:40 PM. Anna made a mental note that Holden left 33 minutes after the Seeing-Eye failed.

"Mister Scarnici, do you know a Mister Owen Holden from Doctor Marks' office?" asked Anna as she motioned towards him.

"Sure do. He came every month or so to check on Mister Vitale's pacemaker."

Anna noted that Holden was the last person signed in to see Rocco Vitale before his body was discovered. She thought a few long moments, then asked, "Mister Scarnici, do you know anyone who might have a key to Vitale's place; someone who's so familiar to you and the security team that they might bypass the sign-in requirement; just walk by in a hurry and gain entry?"

"Sure do. There's only one—his lawyer, Mister Cornado."

Anna looked to her right and left and asked if her colleagues had any questions of Mr. Scarnici. They did not. Anna adjourned the meeting, told Mr. Scarnici to secure the log and make it available on short notice if needed.

The detectives left. Then walked a short distance to Ruben's Sandwich and Salad shop, ordered "take out," walked across the street to a park and found an isolated empty bench. Shanahan was still standing while placing his lunch change in his wallet, when he said. "Damn, I'm going back. The cashier gave me a crisp counterfeit two-dollar bill."

John held up his hand with open palm facing Shanahan. "That bill's genuine. The Treasury just started to reissue them to commemorate the Bicentennial."

As Shanahan settled himself on the bench, Anna spoke, "We've got to learn more about Owen Holden—he might be our man."

"Best way to start is to question Doctor Marks. Holden works for him. Marks should have some helpful background history," said John.

"Good thought. No point in questioning Holden if we don't know much about him," Anna concluded.

"What makes you think that Holden's a suspect?" asked Shanahan.

Anna answered, "He was the last person on the log book to visit Vitale before he was found dead. That's enough for anyone to raise suspicion about foul play."

Shanahan asked, "Anna, could Vitale have been murdered by Holden in some fashion before he signed out of the building?"

"Why not?"

Shanahan glanced towards John, "Do you agree?"

"Perhaps— Perhaps if it was murder by a slow death."

Shanahan asked John for an explanation.

"Well, Vitale must have been alive when Holden departed because the apartment door was dead-bolt locked from the inside. If Vitale died by Holden's hand, he had time to lock the door after Holden left and time to retire to his bed. If murdered, it was by a method that caused a slow death. I have no idea what method that could have been."

"Gosh darn, I forgot that the door was locked from the inside," said an embarrassed Anna.

"Don't worry about it," consoled Shanahan. "Let me summarize what we know and don't know. It's possible that Vitale was murdered by Owen Holden by a method that causes slow death. The agent could be a non-detectable poison; or Vitale might have died from natural causes as Baker, our forensic pathologist, believes. Another possibility is a slow-death murder by someone who did not sign in or out of the building—someone like Joseph Cornado. We can only speculate on Cornado's motive. He had an inheritance to gain."

Shanahan shooed a pigeon away and suggested they finish lunch and question Dr. Thomas Marks another day.

Chapter 13

Thomas Marks received permission from his lawyer, Joseph Cornado, to meet the detectives, but he insisted that the location be at his office after hours. Shanahan suspected that their conversations might be recorded, so he brought along a fountain-pen-sized device that could jam the varied frequencies that were used by eavesdropping machines; frequencies that could not be detected by the human ear. In preparation for the meeting, Anna and John's search of public court records yielded a number of cases in which Dr. Marks testified that accused Davio members were medically incapable of physically committing the crime, or their heart would give out from the stress of trial, or there would be inadequate on-site medical facilities if the defendant was sent to prison. Dr. Marks was a frequent cardiology expert witness for the defense. Perhaps the most favored among attorney Joseph Cornado's stable of experts.

Thomas Marks met the detectives in his plush office conference room. It could comfortably seat as many as eight people. Marks and the detectives sat at a mahogany table. The doctor had the appearance of a wise physician—his greying hair, the need for reading glasses, the air of authority, his greater-than-average height, his soft well-groomed features and the gentle voice that spoke in unemotional measured cadence.

Shanahan looked about for evidence of a recording receiver. If there was one, it was well hidden. Perhaps Cornado acquiesced to the meeting to learn what concerned the detectives about Rocco's death; or if Baker was concerned about foul play because he had not released Rocco's body for burial. Cornado had further cause to be suspicious because Rocco's apartment on the twelfth-floor had not been cleared for occupancy and the building security staff must have notified him—the new building manager—that the detectives viewed the surveillance tapes.

Shanahan activated his pen-like jamming device, then he let Anna direct the questioning to restore her confidence after she blundered in forgetting that Rocco's door was dead bolted from the inside when his body was discovered.

"Doctor Marks, when did you first meet Rocco Vitale— sorry, Joseph Vitale?"

"In 1973, he was referred by his primary doctor, Paul Pedonti, for me to assess and follow his recently placed pacemaker. I've been checking it for several years. "

"Why did he need the pacemaker?"

"I saw a report from the Italian doctors who placed the pacemaker; Mister Vitale fainted either from a very slow heart rate or because his heart stopped beating for too long. He had what we call 'heart block.' The part of Mister Vitale's heart that generates and sends signals for the heart to beat was okay, but the natural pathways that carry the electrical signals were faulty and too few signals got through to the heart's main pumping chambers. When that happens, the heart pump fails to send enough blood to the brain and elsewhere. If the heartbeat stops and isn't restored, there's no oxygen to sustain life."

Anna believed that Dr. Marks looked a little tense; she thought he might relax if he spoke about himself.

"Pacemakers are a new field; when did you get interested in them?"

"When I was a kid, I was fascinated by the power of electricity. A bolt hit a nearby tree during a storm; split and torched it. When I got older, a neighbor was electrocuted fooling around with a fuse box. In medical school, I looked after an unconscious Con-Edison lineman who later said that he was electrocuted after touching what he thought was a 'dead' wire. He was lucky to have lived. Anyway, when artificial pacemakers were developed for medical purposes, I wanted to be part of the action and learn how electricity could be used as a therapy for heart-rhythm disturbances. You know the slogan, Better Living Through Electricity."

Anna observed that Dr. Marks had relaxed during his answer, so she got back to being an inquisitor.

"We understand from the pathologist that Mister Vitale had an uncommon pacemaker. A Sorin Brand that has no support services in the USA. Do you know why the Italian doctors decided to place that type of pacemaker?"

"No idea. I only saw the operative note given to me by Vitale. It was in Italian. I had my technician translate it into English. Why he had a Sorin Pacemaker didn't make sense to me. I have a large assortment of programmers except for a Sorin, but Vitale owned one."

Dr. Marks went on to explain that Vitale would come to the office after hours for a pacemaker check every two months. He came by a private-coach limo service that he arranged. The driver would wait and return Vitale to his building when the session was over. Vitale brought his Sorin Programmer with him and both Marks and his technician would check the pacemaker.

"During a scheduled evening pacemaker check," Marks said, "a young cleaning lady from housekeeping services unlocked the office door with her pass key, wandered in and recognized Mister Vitale. She called out his name. He didn't respond. Then she reminded him, 'Don't you remember? I was a waitress at the Ponte Vecchio Café. You took a liking to me.'

"Vitale still didn't answer. When his color turned even paler than usual, I escorted the cleaning woman out of my office. From that day on, Vitale insisted that all pacemaker checks be done at his apartment by my technician, whom he had gotten to know pretty well."

"Who is your technician? What's his or her name?"

"His name is Holden—Owen Holden."

Anna's strategy had directed the conversation to the main purpose of the meeting with Thomas Marks—to learn about Owen Holden.

"How long has he worked with you and what did you learn about him before you hired him?"

The answer was so rapid and detailed that John and Shanahan, who usually make mental notes, were forced to jot down some remarks on their notepads. Marks told the detectives that Owen Holden was a highly qualified pacemaker technician. Before working in the city, he had worked at the Veterans Hospital in Buffalo, New York, with pacemaker pioneers Chardack and Greatbatch. Holden assisted the pioneering doctors in their animal laboratory, the operating room and during their pacemaker follow-up sessions.

"Out of the blue, I received a call from Holden; he mentioned his qualifications and asked if there was an opening for a pacemaker technician. The timing was auspicious; my far-less qualified technician had just taken a leave of absence to deliver her baby and was uncertain if she would return to the workforce. So I hired Holden. He was terrific. A big plus; so good that he taught me what he had learned from the masters. I don't know why he left Buffalo; he simply said that it was destined that he come here."

Anna inquired about Holden's early life, his background before working in Buffalo.

"He didn't talk much about that," said Dr. Marks before going on with what little he did know. He remembered that Holden was a US Citizen—many medical technicians are not; his father died when Owen was young and he was raised by his mother. They were poor until, by chance, they came into some money. When Owen was in his early teens they moved to Italy, where, with limited financial resources, they could live a more comfortable life as expatriates. He was a bright student and became interested in applied electrical engineering. Dr. Marks concluding remark was, "That's all I know about his past."

Once again, by changing the subject, Anna wanted to break any tension in the air. "We're almost finished; I was hoping I'd get a chance to come back to this beautiful office. Have you been in this building for long?"

Marks said that he had been there a while; even longer than Paul Pedonti whose office was in the same building. Pedonti had referred Rocco Vitale to be a patient and also introduced Cornado as an acquaintance. Before Pedonti settled into the building, Dr. Marks said that he thought of moving to a place that had lower costs. But when Cornado hired him to testify as an expert witness, the added income was more than enough to remain in the building and upgrade the office. Dr. Marks ended his remarks by proudly stating that he was the first-ever cardiology expert witness to be placed on retainer by a consortium of defense litigants.

Anna needed to extract more information. "Was there anything unusual about the last visit that Holden made at Vitale's place on that last pacemaker check?"

"Holden said all was well with Rocco and that the pacemaker's performance was unchanged from the past. I checked its parameter print-out myself. Perfect."

Anna asked, "What was the time and date of that print out?"

"Vitale's programmer has a chronometer. I will look at Rocco's record and tell you the time and date of Holden's print out."

"Well, we might want to talk to him directly. When can we arrange to meet him?"

"You can't."

"Why not?"

"He gave me two weeks' notice and has already left without a forwarding address. Said he'd let me know when he needed a job recommendation. I'm currently reviewing applications for a new technician but don't expect to find one as qualified as Owen Holden."

Shanahan asked Dr. Marks to provide Anna with some contacts to start her search for Owen Holden's whereabouts. Anna was determined to support her suspicion that Holden might have betrayed Rocco, so she asked, "Did he say why he had to leave?"

"No. Only that it was destined that he leave."

Chapter 14

Shanahan complimented Anna on her conversation with Dr. Marks. The team had a lot of new information and even more unanswered questions.

Shanahan summarized the facts:

Owen Holden was the last known person to see Vitale alive and then abruptly disappeared. Holden was well grounded in pacemaker technology. No one could explain why Vitale, an American Citizen on a temporary visit to Italy, would receive an Italian-made Sorin Pacemaker without backup for the pacemaker in America. According to Dr. Marks' records, Vitale's Sorin Pacemaker output parameters were unchanged when checked by technician Holden on March 12, at 2:58 P.M. while it was within Vitale's body. Dr. Baker had specialist Peter Merlino check the pacemaker and its leads as a bench test outside of a human. Merlino found no cause for concern. Perhaps he can clarify why the Italian implanter installed the only Sorin Pacemaker to be found in a citizen of the USA.

Anticipating that Merlino might want to repeat or add some tests to Vitale's pacemaker and wire that remained in his possession, Anna and John went back to Vitale's sealed apartment, had pre-approval to be given passage by the police guard, retrieved the pacemaker interrogator programmer instruction manual and operative note and then made preparations to visit Dr. Peter Merlino.

The date was set; arrangements were made for a meeting that would finally be with a cooperative helper of law enforcement.

Merlino reviewed Vitale's most recent pacemaker in-body printout data. The parameters gave no clue of a problem or an impending problem. The wire was intact and the amount of resistance in the wires had no evidence of an insulation leak or wire break. The pacemaker voltage was set at an adequate level. Too little voltage would not be safe; too much voltage would prematurely deplete the battery.

Peter Merlino was a specialist in heart-rhythm management and electrocardiac therapy. He shocked the fibrillating hearts of dying patients back to normal; he implanted pacemakers and managed complex regimens of anti-arrhythmic drugs. Merlino was an academic, a member of varied specialty societies and a historian of multi-century efforts to tame electricity for the benefit of hearts that lose their proper beat. Saving lives by preventing or treating life-threatening arrhythmias was supported by an international community of dedicated scientists, electrical engineers and clinicians. Leading centers were in Australia, Italy, Sweden, France, England, Canada and many cities in the USA such as Greater New York, Buffalo, Boston, and Minneapolis.

Merlino was fluent in Italian. He quickly read the implantation report and said that Vitale's operation was done in a standard manner. He also said that the Italian implanter, Dr. Joseph Higgins, was well known in the field. There was to be an international pacemaker convention scheduled to start in Manhattan in two weeks. Because the electrophysiology specialty and the criteria for patients needing pacemakers had expanded, Sorin planned to open sales and service centers in the

USA. Higgins was recruited to be an "advance man" for Sorin. He had been, and still was, an investigator and coordinator of many of Sorin's clinical pacemaker research trials. Merlino and Higgins were scheduled to co-host a luncheon panel.

Merlino asked if he could borrow Vitale's pacemaker programmer, instructional manual and operative note. "I will contact Doctor Higgins and have him bring a copy of Vitale's operative note, office record and hospital record. I'm told that Vitale died without family so there is no issue of privacy. Maybe we can learn why Higgins was so insensitive about not placing an American-made brand."

Shanahan agreed to the loan. Anna and John drew up papers to document the temporary loan to Merlino who appeared to be a willing deputy.

Before leaving, Shanahan asked Merlino, "Have you ever heard of a pacemaker technician named Owen Holden?"

"Never."

Chapter 15

Shanahan never took a day off. But he slowed down on Sunday. Sometimes he met a friend for breakfast or lunch. One of the regulars was Mortimer Baker. Sometimes Shanahan went to church services, but he always settled in at his small apartment, sipped a coffee and read an accumulation of newspapers that featured items about national and international news as well as the sensational that featured gruesome suicides and serial killers who left a trademark, like Jack the Ripper's eviscerated victims. There were articles about dead and dying people found in the streets, bodies found in back alleys or woods with crushed skulls—sometimes with brain matter leaking through cracks or bullet holes. There were suspended bodies discovered with a rope around their neck or other bodies lying in pools of blood from life-ebbing tributaries that originated at the site of stab wounds. There were also reports of folks that had simply been called by their maker when their time on Earth was over—when their work in this life was done. Shanahan wondered what his circumstances would be when he took his last breath. Would it be a natural death or a departure by the hand of someone he helped to exile in prison; someone who claimed to be innocent and vowed retribution toward those who thought otherwise?

In the evening, Shanahan read police bulletins, enrolled in criminology educational programs and read classic books. His favorite was *Crime and Punishment* by Dostoyevsky. Shanahan believed that many a vicious murderer ultimately has remorse and confess their sins with hopes of forgiveness by society and their lord.

On this Sunday he eventually focused on the Vitale case. Was Vitale murdered by one of his many enemies or did he have a natural death? By exclusion, a natural death was favored by Mortimer Baker, the forensic pathologist. No suspects, only a couple of "persons of interest." Cornado had a soft motive, but with patience and time, he would eventually gain his inheritance from Vitale's estate. An uninvited Owen Holden, who suddenly appeared at Dr. Marks' door, was the last known person to visit Vitale and then disappeared without an explanation or a forwarding address. Anna was assigned to use all of her ingenuity and intuition to follow his trail; to track him down.

The telephone rang just as Shanahan was asking, "What am I missing?"

The call was bad news. Mortimer Baker had been hospitalized with a massive intra-cerebral bleed. He was on life supports and in a coma. Other than worry and concern for a good friend, there was a sense of urgency. At Shanahan's request, Baker had delayed making a final determination about the cause of Vitale's death. The first official act of Baker's replacement might be to sign the death certificate, an action that would close the investigation. Death attributed to "natural causes" didn't seem right for a known criminal with enemies that lurked around every corner.

The next day Shanahan went to the hospital to learn firsthand about Mortimer Baker's medical status. Shanahan had become emotionally hardened to the eerie atmosphere of an Intensive Care Unit. He'd often been a witness to this familiar scene. On the law-enforcement side, police and detectives at death's door from injuries received in the course of duty or from natural failure of their vital functions. On the criminal side, interrogating injured felons in hospital at the moment they were stable enough to be questioned with their lawyer at their side.

Upon entry to an Intensive Care Unit, a visitor's sense of sight and hearing are the first to be invaded. Those senses imprint on portions of the brain that control anxiety, sadness and helplessness. Visitors often ask, "Will this also be my fate with an array of tangled tubes and wires, emanating from what could too-soon be my corpse?" Determinants of a patient's physiology are represented by varied squiggly lines that move across a monitor screen. The loudest ambient sound that fills the room is from a ventilator with its expanding and contracting bellows pushing oxygen into and withdrawing carbon dioxide from the lungs through a tube that disappears into a patient's mouth. A softer sound is a click that coincided with each heartbeat. Then there might be a frightening very loud klaxon that is an emergency signal for pre-conditioned care-givers to respond because of a life-threatening patient event such as an oxygen level or blood pressure that drifted too low, a heartbeat that stopped or ventilator failure. Luckily, nine times out of ten a monitoring electrode detached or had to be adjusted.

Shanahan was granted just five minutes to sit by Baker's side. Immersed in the moment, he remained calm, spoke some words of comfort, said a prayer and then just sat there in deep thought until the time was up. A nurse escorted him back to the waiting room. Before returning to her patients, she said,

"Detective, only one visitor at a time. If you're staying, I'll let you know when you can see Doctor Baker again."

A woman in dark glasses, seated across from Shanahan, looked up from the open Bible that she was gripping in both hands.

"Have you come to visit my brother, Mort? Are you his friend, Detective Dan Shanahan?"

"I am. How can I help? But first, tell me more about yourself."

With that, Shanahan rose from his chair, and sat next to Dr. Baker's sister.

"My name is Helen. Mort was a loner with very few friends. He considered you among them. There are only the two of us. Neither he nor I ever married. We look after each other. Because of his condition, the doctors and Mort have put me in a terrible position."

"How's that?"

Helen explained that she was Mort's health-care proxy. If Mort could not speak for himself, she agreed to speak for him in matters of his health. The neurologist, Dr. Brownell, told her that Mort had all the clinical signs of brain death. He had fixed-dilated pupils, absence of primitive brain reflexes, inability to respond to simple commands, inability to breathe without a respirator and a nil response to painful stimuli. The prognosis for any type of recovery—even a minuscule recovery of brain function—was highly, highly unlikely. The brain's electrical dynamo had blown up causing the brain to swell so much that pressure within the skull has reached a level that exceeds the blood pressure. So no blood was supplying the brain; no blood equaled no oxygen; no oxygen equaled brain death.

Shanahan held up his hand, "Then there's no hope?"

"That's what Doctor Brownell said. My eyes are terribly swollen from crying. That's why I'm wearing sunglasses. Brownell said that when they have a couple more electroencephalograms—you know, EEGs—that show a brain-wave pattern indicating absence of any meaningful brain activity; they want my permission to remove the life supports from Mort—the ventilator and the intravenous medications that keep his blood pressure high enough to prevent cardiovascular collapse. Mort placed me in a terrible position because I can't agree to remove the life supports. Mort wouldn't want that. Why— Why didn't he take better care of himself?"

"Helen, for me to learn about this is very hard; but why would Mort want to be maintained on life supports if he is in a perpetual coma without an ability to sense anything or respond to anything?"

"Because Mort has a strong belief that death happens when the heart stops beating or breathing ceases naturally or ceases even if artificially assisted. That's generally the view of those that cite scripture. Scripture says nothing about brain waves. To me, Mort looks like he's alive and his God-given soul still resides in his being, so I can't agree to stop life supports."

Shanahan put his hand on Helen's shoulder and reassured her that he now understood. He knew that, medically defined death is failure to breathe; or failure of the heart to beat due to an extinguished electrical spark that stimulates a heartbeat; or the presence of brain waves that meet a definition of brain death that was determined by a panel of scientific experts. But in the State of New York, brain death by EEG criteria is not accepted. In New York, the presence of a non-working severely broken brain is equivalent to a non-working disabled broken finger regarding a body being dead or alive.

At that moment Dr. Brownell entered the room to speak to Helen. Shanahan stood and was about to leave while the doctor and Helen conferred, but Helen insisted that Shanahan remain to give her moral support.

"That's how you can help me," she said.

So he introduced himself to Brownell and returned to Helen's side.

Dr. Brownell immediately got down to business. He told Helen that once the third EEG was completed, Mort would be certifiably dead everywhere in the country except in New York. Here he would be a brainless living corpse taking up scarce space that could help someone with a chance to survive. He said, "The billions of cells that were Doctor Baker's brain are dead. The structure will soon change to liquid jelly."

"Doctor Brownell, if Mort could speak, he wouldn't agree to remove life supports. He would say, 'Do everything you can until my heart stops beating and keep me breathing even if it's by a machine.' Brain-wave death doesn't equate with absence of God-given life."

"I understand your position, but I can't agree. My world is a practical world. Brain-dead Mort will prevent a needy patient from occupying his intensive-care bed. Mort won't improve. Within days or a week his body should suffer irreversible cardiovascular collapse. His heart will stop. He will be dead—a cold corpse by any and all definitions. But, Helen, you're being faithful to his mistaken opinion may cause a retrievable patient being placed in the morgue alongside Mort. Now, will you agree to remove the life supports when the time comes?"

Helen seemed stunned by Dr. Brownell's diatribe. She didn't speak, just turned her head from side to side indicating, "No."

Brownell didn't speak either. He left in a hurry.

"Not a very gentle person," said Shanahan. "I'll visit every day that I can. Mort was, I mean is, a good man."

Gentle or not, Dr. Brownell was right. Mort died four days later. When Shanahan and Helen parted after the funeral, she said, "I know that you and Mort worked together on cases. A few days before his collapse I remember him saying he wanted to explore a theory with you about a mutual case that might have been an unnatural death rather than what he had believed to be a natural death."

Shanahan thought, "That's a perfect fit for Vitale, but what was Mort's theory?"

Chapter 16

While awaiting developments from Anna's search for Owen Holden and any new information from the meeting between electrophysiologist Peter Merlino and his Italian Sorin counterpart, Joseph Higgins, Detective Shanahan sought to find a credible clue about the cause of Vitale's death. He wasn't interested in the phrase "by natural causes," but rather had an interest in "death by premeditated murder." Progress was at a standstill. It was futile to merely think. It was time to act. So Shanahan decided to explore another pathway, as he had done many times during his career. Go to the scene of the crime, assume the mindset of the criminal, linger and observe.

Arrangements were made, approvals and warrants obtained, the day's newspapers purchased, overnight bag packed and a kit of detection tools were all that was needed when Shanahan entered Vitale's twelfth-floor apartment.

After getting settled, Shanahan made a mental checklist of the places to explore in order of importance. He would attempt to open the wall safe behind the fake fuse box in the master bedroom. He would inspect the wired box where the electricians found a blown fuse that caused the corridor security camera to fail. He would once again search for an exit that might allow the murderer to escape the apartment after dead-bolting the entry door from the inside. There was a need to once again search for an obscure hiding place. Then there were the unanswered questions. Who was the murderer? What was the murderer's motive? What was the murder weapon?

The wall safe was large, the front emblazoned with its manufacturer's "Toledo" logo and model number. Shanahan was a patient sleuth. His comrades were not. If they couldn't quickly open it, they would have ripped it out of the wall and blown it up; likely destroying half of its contents in the process. Shanahan would be unhurried, yet efficient. The safe had already been dusted for fingerprints; none matched a registry of known criminal prints other than Vitale's. Shanahan was a proficient safecracker. He had taken courses and had real-time instruction by rehabilitated criminal experts. He subsequently had extensive experience in the field. Shanahan was faced with a dilemma. Should he wear a pair of surgical style gloves that he brought with him to not add his prints to the dial, or should he not wear gloves and wipe all the prints off when he finished the effort? Shanahan decided to add his prints to the dial because a good safecracker relies more on feel than the sound of the disengaging tumblers. He reached into his tool kit for his safecracking needs. Now, Shanahan sat on a chair, positioned the beam of a battery operated spotlight on the dial and secured a combined microphone-speaker on the door of the safe to hear each tumbler release from its locked position. He spun the dial several times to the right, then to the left before deciding in which direction to start. Shanahan suddenly recalled the first lesson he was taught. All safes with the same brand and model number have an identical pre-set combination when sent from the factory.

A small spiral notebook was withdrawn from the tool kit and Toledo-model 1000459 was located. If Vitale did not change the factory-set combination, hours of work would be eliminated. Indeed, the factory-set combination had not been changed. In short order, the safe was opened. With gloves on, Shanahan transferred the contents to the kitchen table. When he finished, there were stacks of uncirculated one hundred dollar bills with sequential serial numbers. Shanahan photographed a group of them to learn if the bills were marked. If so, they would be important evidence about a past payoff or a robbery. Other items included: three handguns with deleted serial numbers; Vitale's passport—each page was carefully photographed; and a diamond necklace on a delicate gold chain.

What remained were two folders of old newspaper articles. The first held clippings about the 1936 disappearance of Vitale's wife and two sons. The second folder contained news clippings about a natural-gas explosion at a private home in Shaker Heights, Ohio, that wiped out an entire family. Leo Lombard, his wife Margaret Lombard and their teenaged daughters, Linda and Joyce, perished in the blast or inferno that followed. A neighbor saw Leo park his car in the driveway, wave a greeting with cigarette in hand, slowly scale the steep front stairs, open the door and be blasted back by the force of the explosion. He landed lifeless on the lawn. An investigation indicated that the gas line at the metered edge of the house had been exposed and breached as it entered the interior. A woman that lived directly across from the Lombards recalled that a uniformed service man from the regional gas company intermittently gathered materials from his marked service truck in mid-morning on the day of the blast—which also shattered her front windows. The utility company had no record of being called to the Lombard home. Foul play was evident. Leo's two brothers posted a reward for information leading to the arrest of the villain. The police believed that gang warfare was the root cause. Leo was an unsavory character. He'd been in prison for a short stay on charges of attempted murder. The evidence was fuzzy and the appellate court reduced the sentence before setting him free. Among the news clippings were blueprints of the structural design of a house including all its water pipes, electric wires, gas lines and a separate list of applicable building permits.

After Shanahan photographed the newspapers, blueprints, necklace and permits, he returned everything to the safe, locked it, spun the dial several times and repositioned the fake fuse box.

In the kitchen, the active fuse box was opened. Each circuit was marked. There were five fuses. One for the master bedroom; another for the guest bedroom and bathroom that was shared by both bedrooms; a third fuse for the living room; a fourth for the kitchen lights, stove, hood, microwave and refrigerator; and a fifth fuse for the security camera located in the corridor. The amperages ranged from 15 to 60, with the solitary 15-ampere fuse serving the dedicated circuit to the security camera and then to the viewing room. Shanahan, of course, knew that fuses blow either from a short circuit or from an overload—so that was an unanswered question.

During the rest of the morning and afternoon, Shanahan had a snack of fruit and a cup of instant coffee. He repeated the search for a hidden exit. Grids were too small. The windows were sealed without a safe approach from above or below the exterior. The ceiling, floor and walls had no hidden egress to another apartment above, below, or beside. The kitchen hood exhaust above the stove had a small-diameter pipe as did both bathroom-floor overflow drains which were there to prevent a flood.

To exclude a missed sealed hiding place, Shanahan once again went through the drill of tapping the walls, ceiling and floor—and to carefully examine the bed mattresses and upholstery of the couch and chairs.

During the evening, the master detective directed his thoughts to the newly discovered revelations found in the safe. Why was Vitale interested in Leo Lombard? The answer might be unearthed after securing permission from the local police to send Junior Detective John Knight to Shaker Heights. Did the police find a person of interest or a suspect? If so, did someone collect the reward? What was Leo Lombard's business? What did his two brothers do? What else could be learned? John Knight would go to Shaker Heights, Ohio, while Anna finished learning what she could about Owen Holden.

After another snack of fruit, cheese and crackers, Shanahan finally read the newspapers of the day then retired early. Some of his best ideas occurred while half asleep—when his mind was uncluttered and focused on an unsolved question or on something that didn't seem right, like the reason the low-ampere fuse blew when it was guarding both an intact camera and circuit to the observation room. Why did the fuse blow in the absence of a short circuit or an "overload" on the system? Shanahan slept on Vitale's couch and on all aspects of the unsolved case.

The next morning he slowly walked about the apartment several times with a compass from his tool kit in hand. Finally, with a spring in his step, Shanahan grabbed his broad brimmed hat and departed for breakfast at his favorite café.

Chapter 17

After Shanahan made some calls related to "unfinished business," he filed a summary report of the case to the attention of his superiors at headquarters; he then contacted Anna for a progress report.

While investigating Owen Holden's leased apartment, Anna inquired about his having friends or his conversing with neighbors. The response was uniform, "Who is Owen Holden? Did he live here?" Holden did not leave a forwarding address at the postal service. Even though Owen occasionally used an internal phone to call the front desk in his "secure building" and even though the front desk received an occasional message from Dr. Thomas Marks to convey to Owen, none of the doormen could agree on his physical appearance or the clothes that he usually wore. There was no record of a telephone rental from the Bell System. Owen Holden was a "loner" either by nature or by design. The landlord got a note from Owen that included three months' rent in advance. He was immediately vacating the apartment. There was no need to refund the deposit even though there had been no damage. It ended with, "Find a new tenant. Sorry for your trouble."

Anna had better luck at the Veterans Hospital in Buffalo, New York. Holden had worked there for four years. The employment office hired him as a phlebotomist to draw blood from clinic patients, hospitalized patients and those who had volunteered for experimental studies. Owen Holden had graduated from a two-year program for medical technicians at an upstate school. He concentrated on the internal operation and needs of medical laboratories like chemistry and microbiology units. At his Veterans Hospital interview, he emphasized a wish to work in the medical department rather than surgery, dental or radiology. When told that the only opening was for a phlebotomist, Owen said that he was well suited for the position because he did not mind the sight of blood. Owen was hired after assurance that he was a law-abiding American citizen.

Owen believed in the ideology of a conscientious objector, but his religion did not permit him to be certified. He would not carry a weapon even if ordered, would not put on a military uniform if asked—but would do his best to help those who believed it was their duty to serve their country. He would be happy working in any hospital. A secondary goal would be to serve his country by working in a Veterans Hospital. Historically many conscientious objectors worked in hospitals during a declared or undeclared war.

After two years as a phlebotomist, his eye must have caught an internal job posting for a research pacemaker technician. That's how he became so expert with this new class of instruments. He learned the science and knew how to apply the science.

Owen was well liked at the hospital and was the first to offer a helping hand to any needy co-worker. He did attend co-worker farewell parties and raised a glass of ginger ale to wish them success. He did not drink alcohol.

Then, without warning, he quit. Owen told the administrator of the hospital that he would supply a forwarding address when he got settled. That hadn't happened.

Anna interviewed Owen's teammates, his supervisors and the scientists and doctors in the laboratory. None knew why he left. None knew anything about him other than his deep interest in liturgical music and his custom of attending church services every Sunday. He was not a member of any church committee. He didn't even go to his church-sponsored Bingo tournaments. Owen was a very private person.

He lived just off the hospital campus. Anna received the same reception at his apartment complex as she had in New York. No friends. Owen never spoke to neighbors. His abutters' only comments were that they heard music through the shared wall with his apartment. There had been a telephone in his apartment that was rented at the lowest rate—outgoing emergency 911 calls only. An authorized check of his phone calls during four years revealed that none were made. He must have used a pay phone for personal calls, perhaps to avoid numbers that could be traced. The landlady had a poor memory of Owen Holden, only that there had been no conflicts and that he left no forwarding address.

Anna was at a dead end, so Shanahan asked her to finalize her report and join John in Shaker Heights. Two could work faster than one. Shanahan added, "We're running out of time."

Chapter 18

While the "fog" was clearing from his sleep-dulled brain, Detective Shanahan asked himself, "What's ringing? Is it the phone?"

Finally he grabbed the receiver, "Hello."

It was Peter Merlino. "Sorry to call so late. You sound groggy. We have to talk. Now—not later. I spoke to Doctor Higgins at today's conference."

"Higgins? Who's he?"

"You know, the Sorin guy from Italy. He did a painstaking check of the Sorin Pacemaker with Rocco's borrowed programmer and a special receiver that he brought with him from Italy. He knew much more about Rocco's pacemaker than is printed in the owner's manual; he left me copies of all the records he had on Vitale and rushed off to catch a flight at the airport." Merlino paused, the line was silent. "Are you there or did you go back to sleep? Listen—Higgins' analysis of Vitale's pacemaker was extremely disturbing. I just finished reading the English translation of Vitale's medical record. I couldn't put it down. It's an absolute revelation. To honor Doctor Baker's memory and his faith in me as an expert in electrical matters of the heart, you must meet me at my office right now."

"Okay, after a coffee, I'm on my way."

Merlino was waiting at the secure entry to the building when Shanahan's taxi emerged from the sparse traffic that travelled during the darkness of night. The cab stopped. Shanahan stumbled out after telling the driver, "Stay; keep the meter running; keep the doors locked; wait till I return. It's not a safe neighborhood at night."

Nothing was said until the doctor and detective settled in the office waiting room. Shanahan spoke first.

"You got me here at this ugly hour, so it better be good."

"It's better than good. I'm sure that I've got answers to some of your questions about Vitale."

Merlino went on to explain the reason that Vitale received a Sorin Pacemaker rather than one that was manufactured in the US. Vitale hadn't arrived on a tourist visa. He came on a business visa; with extensions, he planned to stay in Italy for an indefinite period of time until his business was concluded.

"What kind of business?"

"Vitale didn't say, but while there he planned to contact a long-lost sister and nephew. He never mentioned their names."

"What? He had no sister and his wife had no siblings. Vitale had no nephews."

"Well, that's what he told Higgins," said Merlino. "Anyway, because Vitale planned to stay in Italy for an indefinite duration, Higgins placed a prototype experimental pacemaker that to this day hasn't been released. It has a memory for arrhythmias that can be accessed with a special code; it's dialed in from a Unique Sorin Pacemaker Memory Receiver. Higgins brought one with him when he learned why I needed his expertise."

Shanahan was getting impatient. "You and others already checked out the pacemaker and it was in perfect working order. No deviation from its prior parameters. The beating of the heart couldn't have become critical the same way it did before the pacer was placed. On the other hand, if the heart stopped pumping blood because the main chambers fibrillated, Vitale would have immediately dropped dead from fibrillation or a number of other undetermined 'Natural Causes.' So, tell me, did the pacemaker's heart rhythm memory show fibrillation?"

"I guess you're still half asleep," said Merlino. "No it didn't fibrillate. Listen! Someone shut off his pacemaker."

"What? How's that?"

"The pacemaker memory's accurate. The pacemaker was working fine. Suddenly there's a signal from Vitale's pacemaker programmer that's detected by Higgins' Unique Sorin Pacemaker Memory Receiver. The pacemaker's been totally shut off. The heart doesn't beat because it's totally dependent on the pacemaker. No beats for five minutes. Then there's another programmer signal that restores pacemaker stimuli that can't spark any heart action. The pacemaker's working again, but the heart isn't working."

Shanahan's eyes were wide open. His jaws were locked tight. He was speechless.

Merlino continued, "No heart beat for five minutes. No oxygen to the brain and body. The brain dies, the heart dies, the body dies and Vitale dies. Now is that information worth your coming here in the middle of the night?"

"What about a pacemaker malfunction?" asks Shanahan.

"None like that have even occurred according to Higgins. This happened because the pacemaker was deliberately shut off. It's hard to disable the pacemaker. To shut it off, you've got to initiate a two-step procedure. Another two-step requirement is needed to turn it on when it's in the 'Off' mode. The On-Off directions are in Vitale's standard instruction manual that incidentally does not mention anything about his pacemaker being an experimental upgrade with an arrhythmia memory."

"Doctor Merlino, during the time you've had Vitale's pacemaker, did you shut it off and turn it on?"

"Absolutely not. I've been its custodian since you gave it to me; I locked it up in my desk drawer until examined by Higgins."

"We don't know why Baker thought that Vitale's death might have been unnatural, but now we know how he died. It was deliberate and premeditated murder," said Shanahan.

Merlino handed over copies of the data supplied by Dr. Higgins, and returned Vitale's pacer with its attached wire, programmer, instruction manual and operative note. He asked, "Do you have a suspect?"

"Yes. Don't say a word to anyone; contact Higgins with the same directive; say nothing to my associates. I want them to think it through without being told. They're learning on the job. Vitale's murder will become an important teaching case, if and when we can learn who did it, why they did it and exactly how they did it?" Shanahan put on his hat, thanked Merlino for his first big break in the case, and was escorted out by him to the secure front entrance where the taxicab was still waiting.

Chapter 19

Owen Holden graduated from "a person of interest" in the death of Rocco Vitale to a premeditated murder "suspect." If not for an advanced prototype pacemaker with an accessible memory for unusual heart action and a dramatic pacemaker programming change, the murderer would have committed the "undetectable perfect crime."

Shanahan had a suspect. The pacemaker's heart-rhythm memory printout that was gathered by Dr. Joseph Higgins had no time frames by date or hour—only duration in minutes. To be exact, five minutes without a heartbeat before the restoration of pacemaker function. Without any attempt at cardio-pulmonary resuscitation, the resurrected pacemaker stimuli were ineffective after the five-minute interval that the heart died.

During life, Owen Holden was the last known person to test Vitale's pacemaker. Vitale was found bare-chested in bed. That would be the expected place and dress of a patient during a home pacemaker check. Without a heartbeat for five minutes, the person would be dead in bed and remain bare-chested. All the circumstantial evidence pointed to Holden except that nagging question: How did Vitale's door get dead bolted from within after Holden exited the apartment and the building? There was another unanswered question: What was the motive?

Shanahan called John and Anna in Shaker Heights. They were making slow progress learning what they could about Leo Lombard. Shanahan was eager to learn why Vitale was interested in Lombard, so he decided to join them and caught a flight to Ohio.

Once again the team was together; the junior members asked Shanahan what he'd been doing.

"Mostly thinking and some routine detective work."

Shanahan asked how much ground they'd covered. Anna and John had searched the archives of the local library and newspaper. They retrieved and copied every article about Leo Lombard's death, the explosion and the aftermath.

"The aftermath—did anyone collect the reward?"

Anna answered, "Leo's brothers, Bart and Dom, didn't cooperate. We told them that Leo's cold-case had been reopened. We wanted to learn if anyone came forward with information about the explosion, hoping to collect the reward."

"Anna, sorry to interrupt, why didn't they cooperate?"

Anna continued without answering Shanahan. "Bart the older, a tough guy with bloodshot eyes and a receding hairline, said everyone in town was suspicious of everyone else. He characterized Leo as being a bit rough, a risk taker, a gambler who hated to lose an argument. If he lost a bet—he was sure that he was set-up. Everyone came forward with their suspicions, but no one came forward with anything substantial. Leo, Dom and Bart were partners in a commercial and residential real-estate business. Leo was the outside partner—the public image. He was good looking, a smooth talker and had an easygoing manner. Dom and Bart were the inside operators. Every tenant had a suspicion about who blew up Leo; they often accused each other. Dom, well-tanned, with a ponytail and wearing a multicolored bright Hawaiian shirt, said that he didn't want us to rub salt into his old wounds."

"Too bad, but all may not be lost." Shanahan added, "I'd like to see the newspaper articles. But before I do, where's the next stop on this investigation?"

John answered, "Tomorrow morning we have an appointment at the courthouse archives. It's about Leo and his will. It was contested by his brothers. In the meantime, you can read through the news articles that we retrieved, some are about the will. Leo was a complicated character."

Shanahan added, "After the courthouse, let's swing by Leo's house—the one that exploded."

Shanahan took the thick folder of copied news articles without disclosing that he had already seen some of them in Vitale's apartment.

The next morning, after having a coffee and Danish, Shanahan met Anna and John at the courthouse archives where past cases are available for review by interested parties with cause.

The librarian got the file. When Shanahan saw the title "Lombard vs. Lombard" he muttered, "Huh, that's strange." He opened the file and read page after page. As soon as he finished a page, he passed it onto John who then passed it onto Anna. No one spoke. Once started, a reader couldn't stop.

They had read the entire file by Noon. The librarian was asked to copy it in its entirety and have it ready in 24 hours. For that rapid service they had to pay a premium in advance.

Anna asked, "Where should we go for lunch?" and quickly added, "We can talk about the contested will while we eat. I'm half starved to death."

John volunteered, "I saw a sign, 'New York Style Deli,' on the way over here. It's about two blocks away."

They ordered their preferences, then they hashed over the litigation. The parties on one side were Bart and Dom Lombard; on the other side were two unknowns to the detectives—Lucy and Hugh Lombard. Lucy claimed to be the wife of Leo Lombard and was the mother of his twelve-year-old son, Hugh. If that were true, Leo was simultaneously married to his blown-up family and to Lucy. Poor Lucy, still shaken by Leo's bigamy and his death, testified that she had no knowledge of another wife. If all that were true Leo, with his many other faults, would certainly be sizzling in Hell. According to Leo's will, the beneficiaries in descending order would be his living children, then his wife, then his brothers and last his church.

Twelve years earlier, Leo and his lawyer, Dryden Pappas, drew up what was then a new will. It was written in the strictest defensive legal terms to repulse a challenge. It superseded all previous wills and remained his last will and testament. Attorney Pappas made sure it was properly updated signed and witnessed every few years. Leo kept Dryden informed of Lucy and Hugh's contact information. Dryden and Leo were the only people who knew about the will. The circumstances were "delicate," for Leo was a bigamist and Dryden was his sole confessor. Dryden had the original will and Leo had a copy. When Leo was murdered, Dryden notified Leo's brothers and sole-surviving wife.

The brothers accused Lucy of lying, or, if not lying, entrapping Leo into believing he was Hugh's father. The brothers Lombard didn't believe Lucy's story. It had to be fictitious. It didn't seem possible for Leo to live a double life. If true, they would have had their suspicions. Leo was a risk taker to be sure, but to risk the wrath of two women would be insane.

There was a pause in the chatter among the detectives as a waiter approached with a tray stacked with food that was held up on an edge by one hand, the other edge resting on his shoulder and the other hand outstretched keeping the waiter balanced as he and his cargo advanced on course. The sandwiches were skimpy with only a quarter of a dill pickle on the side, one salad was a mammoth pile of greens sprinkled with chicken, and the other salad was a huge pile of greens sprinkled with tuna fish.

John was dismayed at suggesting they have lunch here. He apologized with the caveat, "Shaker Heights is a long way from New York." The only saving grace was the price. Lunch in Shaker Heights was much less than in Manhattan.

Patrons were sparse at the restaurant, so Anna suggested that they linger over coffee and continue to discuss the litigation.

Leo Lombard met Lucy Nardell in St. John, Minnesota. He was there to purchase a bankrupt shopping mall for his real-estate company; she was a legal assistant working in the office on the day that would finalize the sale from the bank to the Lombard Corporation.

It's hard to know what was on Leo's mind at the time, but taking a page from unfaithful husbands at his stage of life, it might be that he was burdened with the responsibilities of husbandhood, fatherhood and the ever-increasing financial demands of a nagging wife wanting to present the best image to the world of herself and her daughters. Margaret depended on Leo for every little thing. He told his brothers that two tries with

Margaret for a son were enough. The fates had already sent him evidence that it wouldn't happen. He was restless.

Lucy Nardell was a very attractive, well-educated and financially independent woman who had achieved most of her goals. She had always been popular. At the moment she was ready to settle down but there was no one in her love life. In her deposition, she stated that after the property transfer papers were finalized, Leo asked her to be his guest at dinner that evening. He was courteous; he was attractive and he said that he was unattached—so she agreed. They had a good time. Leo left the next day, but said that he'd be back to supervise an upgrade of the newly acquired shopping mall. He made the 700-mile commute from the home office to St. John every couple of weeks. Their friendship blossomed into a romance. The romance led to Lucy becoming pregnant. When several tests confirmed the pregnancy and the certain realization that Leo had fathered the child-to-be, he had no problem proposing that he and Lucy marry. They were in love and the baby should have a father and mother bound by marriage. They took their vows before a Justice of the Peace. Baby boy Hugh was designated on the birth certificate as was mother, Lucy Lombard, and father, Leo Lombard.

Leo was away on business too long and too often. When home, he doted on the baby, saying that Hugh was his good-luck charm. He had a son, a happy marriage and a self-sufficient wife. Lucy was also happy. She was able to care for Hugh full time, was able to work from home part-time and was given enough cash by Leo to live comfortably.

Dryden Pappas paid a visit to Lucy to inform her of the circumstances surrounding Leo's death. As he spoke, she became confused and incredulous. Was she the unsuspecting wife of a bigamist who had lived a double life, a widow and the sole parent of an impressionable young boy who needed his father? When Dryden told her that Leo had left a will and explained its contents, Lucy was even more confused. Leo never appeared to be in financial need. Until Hugh came of age, she would be the custodian of the proceeds from Leo's substantial estate. Lucy was overwhelmed and frightened. Why would anyone want to murder Leo? How did she ever end up in this mess?

Dryden went on to explain that Leo never indicated that he was in danger. He drew up his last will and testament when Hugh was born. The wording of the will was deliberate. Leo believed that his young children would outlive him and their respective mothers, so he listed the word wife rather than wives as a secondary beneficiary.

The testimony of Dryden Pappas crushed the acrimonious assumptions of Bart and Dom. Leo tolerated his marriage to Margaret but was happy in his marriage to Lucy. Leo was the father of Hugh and was ecstatic to be his role model.

The litigation ended in favor of Lucy and Hugh. The Lombard brothers accepted the judgment and offered to help them. After all, they were family. They were Hugh's uncles. All they asked was for everyone to stay in touch.

"Well." said Shanahan, "I just finished my coffee. Good timing. That almost wraps things up. By the way, did you learn anything about the Lombard operation? Was it legitimate?"

John and Anna looked at each other. Anna nodded to John who said, "We were hoping to surprise you. The Lombards are mid-level members of the Sarno Crime Syndicate. Leo was a hit man—an exterminator. Lombard Real Estate, Inc. helped to launder the syndicate's dirty money."

The detectives left the restaurant and drove to Leo's former house—now totally repaired. When they got there, John slowed his rented car, did a drive by and made a U-turn. Shanahan told John to turn into the empty driveway so he could get a better look at the side of the house. After that, they left. On the drive back, John mentioned that he was getting hungry. "That wouldn't have happened till tomorrow if I'd had lunch at a genuine New York Deli."

The next day, they picked up the copy of the transcript at the courthouse and flew back to New York. En route, Shanahan, with an image of Leo's former house in mind that matched the blue print of the house found in Vitale's safe, knew who caused the gas leak. But why and how did the Lombard's deaths fit into Rocco Vitale's murder?

When they deplaned, Shanahan's last words to John were, "Arrange to pick up Vitale's pacemaker stuff at my place and return it to the drawer at his twelfth-floor apartment where it belongs. I'll make the proper arrangements for you to gain passage to the crime scene."

Chapter 20

After the Lombard revelations at Shaker Heights, the investigation stalled. Dr. Peter Merlino had given Shanahan a big break in the case. Now Shanahan needed another break to learn how to connect with Owen Holden. Shanahan knew that his mentees, Anna and John, had been working diligently. They had unearthed valuable information about Leo Lombard and his families. Now was a good time to unwind with Anna and John. So Shanahan planned to have them over for a casual cocktail party. There was a French specialty shop on the West Side that would supply the hors d'oeuvres.

On the appointed day, Anna arrived in an elegant, blue, satin dress. Her eyes sparkled, her diamond earrings sparkled and the glass of champagne in her hand sparkled. Anna was a loner. She felt uncomfortable in social settings. Gatherings among crime-solving co-workers was another matter. There, she could stay focused on the suspects. In other environments, conversations could lead anywhere. The champagne was a comfort. It took the edge off. John arrived a few minutes late. He also chose not to be exactly "casual." He dressed in an unbuttoned undersized black sport jacket, grey slacks, white shirt, a red-and-black striped tie and a red handkerchief protruding from the breast pocket of his jacket. Shanahan was casually dressed in denim dungarees and a New York Yankee pin-striped jersey with the numerals 007 across the back. The trio stood, they chatted for a while and when directed by Shanahan, sat around a low, coffee-colored coffee table with plates and utensils, trays of squab and deep bowls of strawberries. It was self-service except for Shanahan trying not to let the champagne glasses become dry; he was quick to refill from an uncorked bottle nestled among several that were still corked in a stainless-steel bucket of ice.

Shanahan's only conversational prohibition was to avoid the Vitale case.

John asked Shanahan how he kept physically fit. Every cadet was required to pass all the physical fitness tests before graduating from the Police Academy. Beyond that, the only other requirement for those who are issued a police revolver is a refresher course on firearms and the need to demonstrate accuracy. There were no requirements for maintaining physical fitness. Shanahan said that he believed it was important to stay in shape. At home he had a routine of doing sit ups and pushups. He was a member of the YMCA where he sprinted 100 yards and ran a mile around the track. During nice weather, he would jog around the neighborhood with a watchful eye for any suspicious activity. He had gained only five pounds since he graduated from the Academy and never smoked.

John asked the question because he was slipping. He had gained 25 pounds, couldn't sprint without becoming breathless and could no longer run any distance. John could do many pushups but only a limited number of sit ups. "My problem is eating when I get anxious, and this job is stressful."

"Well, start your diet tomorrow, but have another squab and more strawberries right now," said Shanahan as he stood to pile more food on John's plate.

John asked, "Anna, maybe I can get a few tips from you. How do you manage to stay so thin?"

"John, it's a necessity. I can't afford a new wardrobe, so I've maintained my weight, but at the Academy, as you know, I had to pass the same minimum fitness requirements as everyone else. I couldn't have done it without a personal trainer. Today, I'd be dead meat in a struggle to apprehend a criminal." She paused to drain her glass of champagne and then wiped her lips with a napkin imprinted with the Eiffel Tower. As Shanahan refilled her glass, she muttered, "I still have the number of the trainer; I'd better call him."

Shanahan overheard Anna's directive to herself.

"Good idea, Anna; do it. When I was a junior police officer, I had a woman sidekick as a partner in my squad car. Stacy was one of the first women to graduate from the Academy. She was imposing; 5-foot-8, agile and strong. Stacy was a mountain woman; she grew up in the West Virginia Smokeys. One day we got a call from the 911 dispatcher about domestic violence. Not the first time from that address and that apartment. We were nearby and responded. When we entered the place, a bloody battered woman pointed to a room with a closed door and said, 'In there.' I took the safety lock off my gun and kicked the door open; seeing no one I walked in a little, then further. A guy had lifted himself up to the ceiling by holding onto a ventilator grate just beyond the inner side of the door. He let go, plunked down behind me and, rather than attack me, ran out of the room right into the arms of Stacy. He was no match for her. She threw him to the ground and had one arm pinned behind him. He suddenly had a knife in his free hand and stabbed her again and again before I smashed him on the head with the butt of my revolver until he went limp. It all happened in an instant. The pair of first responders that arrived immediately attended to Stacy who was in bad shape. The pair that followed carted off the knifer who was still unconscious. Our back-up police officers brought the battered bloody 911 caller to the hospital and I followed to see how Stacy was faring. The knife punctured a lung and severed an artery. When she got to the hospital she had lost a lot of blood and was barely breathing with only one functioning lung. As soon as Stacy recovered, she requested a transfer to another partner. One who is not as stupid as me. A partner that looks up and all around after kicking a door open. Sometimes we learn the hard way. So, Anna, call that personal trainer, and get strong."

While Shanahan was engrossed in telling his story, Anna had self-served another champagne refill.

"I worry about a couple of things. One is the personal risks of policing the underworld," she said. "The other is if I will ever trust enough to have more than a casual relationship with a guy. You know my father brought shame to my mother and me because he dishonored his police badge. Well, badness is often widespread rather than isolated. He also brought shame to my mother and me by being restless. He disregarded his oath to uphold the law and his vows to be a faithful husband." She paused; before Shanahan or John could change the subject, Anna asked, "Where was I? Oh yes, you know, when we were in Shaker Heights, I didn't give a damn about Leo Lombard being murdered, but felt so sorry for his two daughters and wife Margaret being tangled in his deception, 'cuz I've been there. Then I felt so sad about his surviving wife, Lucy. How in hell can you ever know if a guy's on the level?"

Anna paused again. This time Shanahan seized the moment, "Time for some café au lait and croissants before we call it a day. Anna, is that okay with you?"

"That's okay; sounds good. Don't forget, I'll need a raise for a new wardrobe if you ply me with too many of these great French treats." Then she revealed what had been on her mind for years. "You guys only have to worry about getting killed on the job. I also worry about that. But I have the added worry about ever trusting a guy enough to have a serious relationship, and trusting him long enough to ever consider marriage."

When dessert was devoured and the coffee urn was dry, after goodbyes were concluded and John had volunteered to escort Anna back to her apartment—Shanahan couldn't believe that Anna, John and the champagne had temporarily displaced the Vitale case and the search for Owen Holden from his mind. Shanahan realized that the remaining champagne would be a further distraction. So what?

"Might as well polish off what's left in the open bottle before getting back to Vitale in earnest."

Chapter 21

John and Anna were on an extended lunch break. It was midsummer. It was pleasantly warm. As a treat, they went to Tavern on the Green in Central Park. John remembered every word of Anna's "confession" at Shanahan's get together: About not trusting men; about her being insecure in most any relationship —even a casual one. The outdoor tables were widely separated. Many were empty. The situation was unusual for New York; John and Anna could talk without being overheard by others. They had privacy. After they ordered their meals, John wanted to talk.

"Because of what you and your mother went through with your father, I can hardly blame you for not trusting guys. Everyone has very private experiences or thoughts; not easily shared with others. You shared some of your private thoughts when we were together at Shanahan's party."

"The champagne had something to do with that"

"My point is that people really don't fully know each other. There's always a hidden portion no matter how long they've been acquainted."

"Are you telling me that you're a man of mystery?" asked Anna as her service pick pierced a piece of shrimp cocktail.

"There are some things, I've never told you."

"I don't want to hear anything about your past or present love life. I'm open to anything else."

"Okay, you eat and listen while I tell you how lucky I was to recuperate from my injuries in Nam and to be talking with you now."

102

While Anna listened and slowly ate lunch, John told her that his resumé was accurate as written, but much had been purposely left out. For many reasons, the Vietnam War was unpopular. One of the most valid reasons was the killing of civilians by our soldiers. The antiwar movement escalated when activists saw published color photos of blood-soaked civilian bodies taken by independent war journalists. The military didn't keep an official count of civilian deaths and injuries. Everyone knew that there were too many that weren't just collateral damage from shelling and bombing. Unarmed defenseless old men, young and old women and children and babies were massacred because they were mistaken for combatants. Journalists saw it happen on a big scale and were compelled to expose the acts to their editors. It would have been easier to remain silent.

John told Anna that after his transport truck hit a land mine, he had near-total backward and forward memory loss and what he was about to tell her was a construct from his hospital and medical records.

"The records said that I saw innocent civilians butchered on a small scale. Any scale in any war is too big. I was there. Being expert in demolition, there were buildings with unknown contents that I had to safely destroy. I wasn't needed for the small thatched huts or homes that our troops set on fire, not knowing if people were inside.

"In defense of our boys, they were under orders to kill everyone and everything in some of those small villages because the villagers were believed to be Viet Cong sympathizers; were harboring the enemy, or were combatants in civilian disguise. A totally destroyed village without crops, potable water, chickens or livestock would not provide sanctuary to the enemy. Our soldiers were following orders issued by their bosses—their commanders—who in turn received their orders from the generals at the top of the chain. It's difficult to judge our guys' response to what they believed to be life threatening. The Viet Cong was an elusive enemy. Too often, our orders were based on faulty intelligence."

John stopped talking and looked into space as if he had been transported back to a Vietnamese village. He swallowed hard, looked at Anna and said, "Not the best topic to bring up during lunch. Is it okay to continue?"

"John, it's just fine. Go on, get it off your chest."

John took a drink of water, looked at the skimpy remains of his weight-reduction salad and continued to summarize what was absent from his resumé.

"The health-record construct said that during a lucid moment, I recalled that the troops were angry. They had lost buddies who were killed by snipers, killed by small mines meant to maim or wound or cause limb loss rather than kill, and they were angry when the Viet Cong attacked at night, only to vanish at daybreak into their familiar territory—perhaps sequestered in the nearest village."

Anna finally spoke, "Couldn't you detect and destroy those small mines and prevent some of those deaths and injuries?"

John told her, "Most mines were cased in bamboo tubes; an explosive within, an inward-turned nail at the bottom to penetrate and spark the explosive. The tube was covered with wax to hold it all together in a waterproof seal. If something weighing more than 70 pounds landed on the soil directly above the mine, the devise would explode. Other models of so-called anti-personnel mines would explode if moved in any direction—that was to prevent them being removed. The flimsy home-made Vietnamese mine-bombs were unreliable; some never exploded —others spontaneously exploded.

"Mines have always been a big problem. During the Second World War, in some occupied countries, the Nazis forced civilians across fields—to be killed while detonating the mines buried by the resistance or placed by their own militia.

"We had a humane method to detonate the Viet Cong mines that lowered our risk of injury and that of our troops. We had bomb-sniffing dogs. I was a handler. The dogs were trained to smell explosives. They weighed too little to detonate a buried mine, but they and I were subject to sniper fire. I would let my dog loose; he, dressed in a canine bullet-proof vest and me in a vest and with a high-powered listening receiver. He was directed into a suspect area and would growl twice when a land mine was located; then he would move on and repeat the exercise until we had a map of the mine field. My sniffer would return on a cue from a dog whistle. We would clear everyone from the area before saturating it with bombs or shells. In theory, all the mines were detonated and were no longer a threat to our troops.

"An occasional villager hiding or sleeping in the mine field was killed. That wasn't a problem, but the fact that the villagers knew where the mines were buried, and didn't let our troops know, infuriated our side every time a buddy stepped on one. The villagers had to know where the mines were. They went to market, they visited families in other villages, they tended their crops and they carried water from distant wells. Resentment builds; it escalates into a reign of terror or culminates into large and small massacres.

"The medical records say that I saw civilians on their knees, hands held together while pleading for their lives with guns at their heads. According to the record, I saw wounded civilians crying out for help; some with loss of limb still attached to their trunk by a ribbon of flesh, others with blood pouring or spurting from within. They got no help other than being put out of their misery with a short blast from an automatic weapon.

"Anna, I thought I understood what was happening, but I couldn't handle it. Deep down it was criminal. How could anyone believe that a baby or an infant was a threat—an enemy that would kill if not killed? When you're a soldier and ordered by your boss to do something against your nature, you probably do it. When everyone in your company is ordered by a superior to do something against your conscience, it's hard not to go along with your buddies. A few courageous guys didn't follow orders, some didn't fire their weapon and more didn't aim at the intended target.

"The record says that images of dead and dying villagers were ever present in my mind's eye. I couldn't sleep at night and couldn't function during the day. I made some mistakes handling explosives. Luckily, no one was hurt. After being relieved of duty, en route for rest and medical care, our transport truck hit a mine. Now multiple physical injuries and new images of dead and dying companions who were in the blown-up truck with me caused me to be totally disoriented. I wasn't sure who I was or where I was but I had a lucid moment when I remembered the medics patching together a friend on my demolition team who was sitting opposite me on the transport truck. The blast ripped Lou's uniform and abdomen open. The medics pushed his guts back inside where they belong and plastered dressings over his abdomen to seal the fissure. One side of Lou's head and face was caved in. A helicopter with medics picked up the living and brought Lou and me to an evacuation hospital. After being stabilized, I was sent up the chain of hospitals until I ended up at Walter Reed for specialized body and mind care to help me overcome what would now be diagnosed as Acute Traumatic Stress Syndrome."

Anna smiled and said, "Let's take a break and get some iced coffee. Then you can finish your story"

Sipping coffee, John eventually continued.

"I was in bad shape with fractured bones, a spinal-cord injury and a mind that constantly focused on scenes of slaughter —slaughter of defenseless people being treated worse than animals. Other scenes flashed of companion soldiers who were in worse shape than me.

"My record says that I screamed and my body shuddered every time a paraplegic, hemiplegic or quadriplegic came into view or each time I saw an amputee. I became withdrawn and depressed. The televised news was as much about the anti-war movement as about the war. Guys on leave from the service were harassed, spit upon and called baby killers. Hardly anyone thanked the soldiers for being patriotic; for serving their country; for risking their lives. There were exceptions. At a Kent State anti-war student protest, counter protestors were heard to say 'It serves them right,' after anti-war protestors were shot by the National Guard. Some were killed, others wounded.

"Anna, I had another terrible lucid moment when a patient on my hospital ward called out my name. I didn't recognize the chap. It was Lou, my demolition team buddy. Half his head and face was full; the other half was indented. He had a prosthetic leg. His appearance was grotesque. I visited him every day. Lou knew he wasn't the same person and was down in the dumps. After many reconstruction facial surgeries, he didn't even care about his appearance. Lou had other operations. Most of his bowel was removed. Our bodies manufacture solid and liquid waste that's eliminated in natural ways. Lou's solid waste passed into a stoma disposable bag attached to his repaired abdomen. When his prewar fiancé came to visit, she recoiled at first sight, fled and never returned. Lou was in physical and emotional pain. The medications provided little relief. He spoke of suicide. Psychiatrists tried a number of failed treatments. Lou told me he wouldn't take his own miserable life even though in death he would finally be at peace. In his religion, suicide is a sin that could not be pardoned at an individual's last judgment. Lou told me that, 'Vietnam was Hell on Earth when we were there. As long as I keep the faith, I don't want to risk going to Eternal Hell.' Lou's faith failed. They found him in a pool of blood. He cut his jugular with a razor blade. After he became another statistic, we were all issued electric razors.

"My record says that the worst moments of my recovery came when I was depressed and having a recurring image of a mound of murdered villagers. On top was a bloodied Vietnamese young girl whose mouth slowly opened and closed. I imagined she was saying: 'Shame. Kill. Mercy. Why? Help.'

"I locked myself in a bathroom and imagined that I was a prophet in the Holy Land. I wouldn't come out until the War Lords came to terms; until they repented; until they signed a peace treaty; until the Canaanites, Amorites and Israelites turned their swords into plowshares. Until then, I would fast and only drink water from the tap. After two hours the authorities broke the door down with a battering ram and restrained me. Antidepressants didn't help. That horrible psychotic episode might have been a blessing because the next treatment was electroconvulsive therapy. They strapped me down, put electrodes on both sides of my head, gave me a short-acting muscle-paralyzing agent and sent an electric shock through my brain. The shock waves scrambled my bad memories and lifted my spirits. I had four treatments. After the last, I was emotionally steady. No more involuntary painful thoughts of Vietnam. All the bad images of the war were erased by electric jolts to my brain.

"Anna, if not for the medical records, I wouldn't know much about what happened to me."

Anna remained attentive during John's journey back to the past.

"John, you went through a terrible time, but I think you're a better person because of it. You're one of the good guys. Your parents raised you to be ethical: 'To do unto others.' You're trying to make the world a better place. You're preventing the predators from destroying the livelihood and lives of the innocent. I'm glad that you confided in me. I'm proud to be working with you and Shanahan. Now it's time to get back to the office."

Chapter 22

Shanahan had made some progress on the Vitale case, but there were no new revelations; just the same bunch of unanswered questions. Why did Rocco Vitale apply for a business visa rather than a tourist visa when he entered Italy? Why did he claim to be searching for fictitious persons? Why did Owen Holden evaporate into "thin air"?

The higher-ups were about to assign a new case to Shanahan when the second big break came. Both Dr. Thomas Marks and the Personnel Office of the Buffalo Veterans Hospital received a request to evaluate Owen Holden's character and work during his employment. Owen had applied for a cardiac-research position at the Boston Veterans Hospital. Shanahan contacted the hospital, explained that Holden was a person of interest and asked and received the address where he was staying in Boston and a head-shot photo. With preliminary warrants secured, Shanahan gathered his team and headed for Boston.

Holden was living at the very posh Copley Plaza.

After checking into an affordable nearby motel, the detectives contacted Holden, and thirty minutes later were joined by him in a small private meeting room that they had secured, just off the main lobby.

Owen Holden's general appearance had not changed from the recording on the security camera when he arrived and left Vitale's apartment: clean shaven, long black hair and deep set eyes.

Anna started the questioning. She would be the least threatening if Holden had anything to hide.

"Are you aware that Rocco Vitale died?"

"No."

"He was found dead in bed and you are the last known person who visited him for a pacemaker check."

"He was perfectly well when I last saw him. Why are you questioning me?"

"As I said, we believe you were the last one to see him alive. We just want to know if he said anything to you about feeling poorly; about being frightened or about being threatened."

"Oh, I see. Mister Vitale was not a well man. Yet everything seemed as usual."

"Thank you, Mister Holden. Now my colleague John has some questions," said Anna.

John was seated directly opposite Owen Holden. Their eyes met.

"Why did you abruptly leave New York without a forwarding address?"

Holden's gaze did not waiver. His steely eyes continued to stare through John's.

"When I was a youngster, I was strengthened by my mother's faith and example. I believe that whatever happens in my life is more or less predetermined. That's the way it's always been. You ask why I did not leave a forwarding address. First, I got a 'calling' to come to Manhattan. Then, when I was settled, I got a 'calling' to apply for a job with Doctor Thomas Marks. After a while, I got a 'calling' to leave. I wasn't sure in what direction I would travel, so I couldn't say where I would be."

"You don't seem to be the type that drifts around. So, where did you go?"

"I went to visit my mother in Australia."

"After that?"

"I went to Canada. You know I'm interested in pacemakers. Researchers at the Banting Institute were the first to electronically pace from within the heart. I wanted to visit that historic location."

John and Holden's eyes remained locked.

"Now you're here in Boston. Why here?"

"There's so much medical history here; so many medical pioneers in pacing and heart problems. I got a 'calling' to come and work here. When I get a job, Boston will become my home."

"You mentioned visiting your mother in Australia and her giving you strength through her faith. Were you raised in Australia? I don't detect an Aussie accent."

For the first time Owen Holden dropped his gaze. He stood and said, "I'd like a glass of water." With that he slowly walked over to a table laden with coffee, bottles of soda, a pitcher of ice water and refreshments. He poured himself a glass of water and slowly returned.

"I was raised in the States. My father died when I was twelve and my mother raised me. She never re-married."

John sensed that the last question made Holden uncomfortable. His eyes shifted, his body tensed and he paused to think.

"Mister Holden, if you need a break, we can finish our conversation at another time on another day."

"I'm fine, we can continue. You're just doing your job."

"Okay, where in the US was your home when your father died?"

Holden's eyes shifted again. He took a long sip of water. Then he answered, 'Minnesota.' "

John persisted, "What city?"

"Saint John."

Shanahan replayed that exchange in his mind again: "What City?" "Saint John." He motioned to John and took over the questioning.

"Mister Holden, you said that your father died when you were twelve years old; that you were raised by your mother and that she never remarried. What was your father's name?"

"Leo."

"Leo what?"

"Leo Lombard," answered Owen, with a slight change in the pitch of his voice.

"And what was your mother's full name?"

"Lucy Lombard."

"Now Owen, how come you are a Holden and not a Lombard?"

After Owen crossed his right leg over his left knee, his foot started to shake.

"It was a terrible time for my mother and me. We wanted to start a new life; a brand-new life. She didn't have much of a support system in the States, so we went to live with friends in Italy."

Owen stopped; said no more. Yet, his foot continued to move to and fro and his eyes blinked—blinked frequently.

"Owen, you forgot to tell me about your name change."

"As part of the plan to start a new life—an entirely new life, we changed from Lombard to Holden."

"Where in Italy did you live?"

"Milan."

Shanahan got up and stood straight as a rod. "Anna, please read him his Miranda Rights. We haven't recorded any part of this conversation. Everything that Owen has told us is certifiable. Name changes are a matter of public record. International travel is recorded. Passports and visas are issued and recorded. Mister Holden, I know more than you think I know. You not only changed your last name, you also changed your first name. You will need the help of a lawyer."

With puzzled looks, Anna and John glanced at each other; then Anna reached into her brief case. She gave Owen a copy of his Miranda Rights and read it to him from another copy.

"What wrong doing are you accusing me of? I've done nothing, absolutely nothing wrong. I don't need a lawyer."

"Owen Holden, you are a suspect in the murder of Rocco Vitale."

"Are you crazy? He was perfectly well the last time I saw him. As a matter of fact I heard him bolt the door after me when I left."

"Mister Holden, you are under arrest. We're going directly from here to the nearest police station to book you. For your own benefit, I suggest that you engage a lawyer sooner than later."

Chapter 23

Owen Holden was booked without bail because he was a flight risk with a mother in Australia, acquaintances in Italy and more than one phony passport.

John and Anna wanted to know what Shanahan knew that neither they nor Owen knew.

"I'll tell you in due time, until then, don't think about what is, think about what Owen Holden might know that we don't know."

John's mind was elsewhere. "Can we think about that while we go sight-seeing here in Boston? I'd like to do that before returning to New York."

"John, I'm one step ahead of you," said Anna. "That's what I was thinking when I got three tickets for tonight's baseball game at Fenway Park."

"Well, Anna, if you're interested in seeing a team that has a bunch of ancient arthritic players like the Red Sox, you must be interested in 'old.' So, let's hop on the subway and have lunch at the Union Oyster House. It's the oldest restaurant in the country; dates back before the Revolutionary War," said Shanahan.

It was a good meal and a good game. Shanahan avoided any talk about the case—claiming they needed to unwind. But, as always, he was thinking of the younger members of his team and wanted them to try and figure things out for themselves.

After extradition from Boston to New York, Owen was transferred to a holding cell in Manhattan. He called Dryden Pappas back in St. Paul, Minnesota, for legal advice. Pappas referred the case to the New York law firm of Goldman, Shea and Fonesca. The senior partner, Ben Goldman, became lead council for Owen Holden. The main arguments in Owen's favor were his stated innocence and no apparent motive to harm Mr. Vitale who was intact when Owen departed from their last meeting.

During the discovery phase of the case, the lead attorney for the prosecution, Salvador Verino, after consultations with Shanahan, would argue at the trial that Vitale was a member of an organized crime syndicate and that there was evidence that Vitale's implanted Sorin Pacemaker had been temporarily programmed to the "off" position for five minutes before being reprogrammed back to its original settings by Owen Holden who was the last known visitor to Mr. Vitale.

As far as a motive—there was deadly competition between Rocco Vitale's Davio Syndicate and Leo Leopold's Sarno Syndicate. In all likelihood, without confirmation, many years ago, some person or persons from the Sarno gang killed Vitale's wife and two sons. Later they bombed Vitale's apartment. Likewise, someone from the Davio gang blasted the life out of Leo Lombard and his Shaker Heights family. Organized crime doesn't subscribe to society's laws. They have their own rules called THE CODE. Organized criminals adhere to THE CODE. It's not "live and let live." It's "kill or be killed." In the end there are no winners. Owen's father was murdered. The prosecution believes that Owen knew that Rocco Vitale was his father's executioner. THE CODE demands retribution, Owen was the Sarno mob's agent in doing just that. He was duty-bound to do so.

When the trial started, fourteen jurors were impaneled, six women, six men and two alternates in case there was an untoward event among the original twelve. The presiding judge was Anthony Tello; head tilted forward, chin tucked into his black robe, upper eyelids at half-mast and overhead lights reflecting off his totally bald head gave him the appearance of being detached and sleeping while presiding over the litigants as they did battle. Judge Tello was born too late. He would have been better off as white wigged during the era after the Revolutionary War.

Shanahan and his team sat just behind Prosecutor Verino and his assistants. Verino stood straight when he faced the jury. He had grey hair about his temples, a deep bass voice, spoke in brief full sentences and emphasized important points by lowering his voice and waving a fist in the air. His strongest argument for Owen Holden's guilt was Rocco's pacemaker memory documenting that the life-sustaining electronic device had been purposely programmed to shut off for five minutes. Only Owen Holden could have done that. Vitale owned and regarded his pacer programmer to be a life-sustaining priceless treasure. He would only permit a trusted person to use it; a person such as Owen Holden.

Salvador Verino called Dr. Peter Merlino, the electrophysiologist, as an expert witness and also had a statement placed in the court record labeled Exhibit A from Dr. Joseph Higgins, the Sorin Pacemaker expert. Exhibit A verified Vitale's pacemaker as a prototype model that secretly had, but was not stated to have, an accessible proprietary print-out memory of hazardous situations. Salvador Verino emphasized that Owen

Holden was unaware that he might leave a paper trail. The damning pacemaker heart-rhythm memory print-out paper trail was Exhibit B.

Ben Goldman—of average height, grey bearded and in a wrinkled grey suit—cross-examined Peter Merlino. Goldman slowly paced back and forth in front of the jury as he tried to convince them that the print out of a five-minute pacing absence was a glitch in the pacemaker's electronic memory. The system was a prototype. All prototypes are in early development and unproven. That Owen Holden had shut off the pacemaker was also unproven. Later in the trial, Ben Goldman planned to call his own pacemaker experts to support his point. But he knew that on cross-examination by Verino they would admit that they had never seen nor worked with Vitale's Sorin prototype model and if they had, they couldn't interrogate its memory. The pacemaker was never released and the Unique Sorin Memory Receiver was in Italy under lock and key to prevent industrial sabotage.

Ben Goldman's time would soon come to occupy center stage while defending Owen Holden. His better argument would be that Owen Holden's last visit with Vitale ended with the usual farewells, Owen being escorted to the door by Vitale and Owen hearing Vitale bolt the door shut. It was a fact that Mike, the building superintendent, and Joseph Cornado broke the deadbolt to enter the apartment.

Prosecuting attorney Verino had just finished his speculative argument about Holden having a motive for murdering Vitale when defense attorney Goldman objected on grounds of "hearsay."

"Sustained," bellowed Judge Tello.

Just then, an associate of Verino burst into the courtroom, ran down the aisle and handed him a note. After a brief conversation with Shanahan, Verino requested a sidebar conference with the judge. A recess was called. Judge Tello, now wide awake, wanted to know what in God's name was so important to interrupt the flow of this murder trial. Verino explained that it was about the door to Vitale's apartment.

"Our forensic detectives had it undergo full X-rays. The wooden door had odd metallic rods in the lower panel. A mechanical industrial engineer had been experimenting with the door and had just solved the mechanism that allowed the lower panel to be removed and replaced. The size of the panel, when removed, would easily permit a full grown man to crawl through into the apartment and out of the apartment. When replaced, the panel was once again "rock solid."

"You've got a nerve to introduce this trick door, probably used by a magician during his vaudeville act in some bygone era," said an agitated Ben Goldman. He then added, "What's this got to do with the present, with my client Owen Holden? Your Honor, you shouldn't permit the door to be introduced as evidence, so long after the discovery phase of the trial."

"That's for me to decide," answered Judge Tello. "Verino, what's the door have to do with Owen Holden?"

"Your Honor, let me briefly outline the State's view of how Owen Holden murdered Rocco Vitale. Holden shuts off Vitale's pacemaker. After Vitale dies in bed, Owen, who had been in Vitale's apartment many times with ample opportunity to "case the joint," opens the fuse box in the kitchen and replaces the dedicated good fuse to the security camera in the hall with a blown fuse. He then dead bolts the front door from the inside, removes the lower panel of the door, crawls out, replaces the panel unseen by the disabled security camera and exits the building.

Judge Anthony Tello reconvened the jury, told them to remain at home for three full days without reading newspapers, listening to the radio, watching television or speaking to anyone about or related to this trial. "Today is Thursday. The prosecution has some new information; both they and the defense need time to study the evidence, prepare their arguments and select their witnesses. They will work over the weekend. We will reconvene in three days—on Monday."

His gavel slammed down and the trial was adjourned.

As Shanahan and Sal Verino's team exited the building, Verino whispered to Shanahan, "We must talk."

Immediately, Anna also whispered to Shanahan, "What else do you know that John and yours truly don't know?"

Chapter 24

The trial resumed on schedule. The prosecution continued to hammer away. Salvador Verino shredded any possible argument by the defense that the blown fuse or the door was an irrelevant incidental finding. His first witness was an industrial electrical engineer who testified that there were no conditions that should have caused the dedicated fuse that serviced the surveillance camera to blow out. The electricians that replaced the blown fuse also testified that they simply replaced it with a new fuse, but found no condition to cause a fuse in that circuit to blow.

On cross examination, Ben Goldman tried to elicit a possibility that the original fuse was defective. But he was told by the electrical engineer and electricians that defective fuses fail early, this fuse was the original, had protected the circuit for decades and should continue to do so indefinitely.

Then Salvador Verino had the door wheeled into the court room. He designated it as Exhibit C and the X-rays of the door as Exhibit D. The mechanical industrial engineer, Harrison Hadley, demonstrated to the jury how the lower panel of the door could be locked and unlocked by a complicated, yet user-friendly mechanism that only required a strong magnet. The metal locking mechanism was on metal rails. A strong magnet could slide the mechanism from its locked position to its freed position. Once freed, the panel could be removed. Hadley wore dark brown-framed bifocal eye glasses with a heavy band around the back of his head that attached to each bow. He was thin and agile. After unlocking and removing the lower door panel by sliding a large magnet from the hinged frame towards the middle of the lower panel, he quickly crawled through the space to the other side, returned through the same space, replaced the slotted panel and moved the magnet from the panel's center back towards the side that held the hinges of the door. He rose, smiled, adjusted his eye glasses, kicked the panel, walked to the other side and kicked it again. It didn't budge. After that performance, Harrison Hadley returned to the witness chair.

Ben Goldman and Bible-clutching Owen had a brief conversation. Then Ben strode toward Harrison Hadley, looked him in the eye through the lenses of his glasses and asked, "How long did it take you to figure out the mechanism that locks and unlocks the panel?"

"A week. Exactly seven days."

"Have you ever seen a door like this before?"

"Never. If I had, with the help of the X-rays, I would have opened the panel in a flash."

Goldman detached from Hadley and quickly walked toward the fourteen jurors. He resumed his slow pacing in front of them dressed in the same unbuttoned wrinkled jacket. His baggy wrinkled pant legs slowly moved one before the other. Finally he stopped, faced the jury and asked, "If it took an expert seven days to solve the locking mechanism of a magician's one-of-a-kind trick door, how could you possibly believe my esteemed opponent's fantasy that Owen Holden, a mere technician by training, could duplicate the performance of Mr. Hadley that you have just witnessed? If he could, Owen Holden would not only be a technician, he would be a psychic."

On redirect questioning, Salvador Verino, asked Harrison Hadley if any tool other than a strong magnet was needed to open and close the lower panel of Rocco Vitale's door.

"As I demonstrated, a magnet is the only tool."

"Mister Hadley, among your special areas of interest, are you familiar with pacemaker technology?" asked Verino.

"Yes I am."

Sal Verino subtly led Harrison Hadley to establish that Owen Holden, as a pacemaker technician, would have strong magnets in his tool kit. In fact, most pacemaker interrogators have a built in magnet to unlock the pacemaker circuits that permit reprograming of pacemaker rate, the electrical strength of each artificial pacemaker pulse beat and the duration of each pacer beat. Owen Holden had a strong magnet, the essential tool to open the door panel; the only other thing he needed was the knowledge.

With that, the prosecution rested its case. Now it was Ben Goldman's turn to call his witnesses for the defense. His strongest arguments had been undermined. Although Ben Goldman's objection was sustained when Verino speculated that Owen Holden had a motive to kill Rocco Vitale, the jury heard that Holden somehow knew that Vitale murdered his father. The court stenographer had deleted the words from the record, but couldn't scrub Verino's words from the memory of each juror. The print-out recording that the pacemaker had been shut off on purpose was a hard fact and the removable door panel cast doubt that Vitale was well enough to deadbolt the door after Owen departed. The door could have been dead bolted by Holden before he crawled through the bottom panel to exit the apartment.

The morning hours had passed quickly. Before Judge Tello called a recess for lunch, the outlook for Owen Holden looked grim and he knew it.

When the trial resumed, Ben Goldman faced Judge Anthony Tello, instead of the Jury. "Your Honor, my client is considering changing his plea."

That short sentence drew a long-loud cacophony from the observers, the press, and the jurists.

Tello jumped up, smacked his gavel on his desk instead of the sound block; in his excitement he overlooked the badly damaged desk and shouted, "Order. Order in the court."

When quiet and decorum were restored, Ben Goldman continued.

"Against my advice, my client is considering changing his plea—but only if he can first take the stand and tell his side of the story. His reasoning is complex, so much so, frankly, I believe that he can do a better job than me in presenting the reasons for his actions. I know this is irregular, Your Honor. Highly irregular. But, to save time and get to the truth—may we proceed?"

Tello swallowed and blinked his eyes. He looked at the jury. He looked at the defendant. He looked at Goldman. Then he uttered a single word.

"Proceed."

Owen Holden stood, was sworn in with a hand on his own Bible, and then sat in the witness chair.

Ben Goldman appeared even more downtrodden and wrinkled as he asked Owen Holden to briefly describe what it was like at age twelve to know that his father was murdered.

"First let me say, that until the prosecution presented information that I did not know existed, I believed that I had committed the perfect crime and was certain that I would get away with it, so I told Attorney Goldman that I was innocent. That was until today's lunch break when I told him the truth. Now let me tell you what my life has been like since my father was murdered."

Owen Holden told the jury that his mother and Leo Lombard were very much in love, that Leo had been a wonderful, attentive, devoted father and that his mother was still in "shock" after learning about the circumstances of her husband's murder. Leo was a member of the Sarno Crime Syndicate. Their long-term rival had been, and remained, the Davio Syndicate. Crime syndicates embed all types of spies, agents and informants into the workings of rivals. Retribution is an important part of THE CODE of syndicated gang justice. The Davios believed that Vitale's wife and sons were kidnapped and murdered by Owen's father who was a young Sarno at the time. According to THE CODE, retribution demanded that the Davios destroy Leo Lombard, his wife and all his known children. If he were willing, that honor belonged to Rocco Vitale, the sole remaining member of his family. Rocco had another unrelated score to settle, for it was understood that the Sarno Gang tried and failed to kill him many years earlier when they bombed his apartment.

Owen had been speaking for a while. He stopped, paused, drank from a glass of water, and then continued to tell his story to the jury.

Shortly after his father was killed, his mother was told that the Davio executioner would learn that Leo had another child and another wife, that there had been incomplete retribution, that she and her son must disappear and change their names.

They moved to Milan, Italy. Newly minted Owen Holden, formerly Hugh Lombard, was devastated by the loss of his father. He never reclaimed the love and affection that Leo had bestowed on him. Owen's mother was very religious and observant. She made sure that he too followed in the tradition of her religious teachings, especially performing acts of brotherhood and good will to all. So Owen told the jury that he rejected violence, became a pacifist and adopted the principles of a conscientious objector.

The Sarnos kept mother and child informed. After about six years, they were told by the Sarno Gang that Vitale was the one who killed Owen's father. The Sarnos would track Vitale's movements. Owen and his mother should stay put in Milan. They would be safe there unless Vitale or some other Davio came to finish the job—to kill Owen.

When Owen was eighteen years old, they got word that Vitale was coming to Milan to find them. He would be looking for Lucy Nardell Lombard and her son named Hugh Lombard. Vitale's mission was to execute Owen. Lucy might also die in the process as collateral damage.

Owen turned sideways in the witness chair and spoke directly to the judge hoping to be fully understood.

"Mother and I split up. She went to Australia and I returned to the States. Once again the Sarnos told us to be ultra-cautious and let them know our whereabouts. Years later, when I was working at the Buffalo Veterans Hospital, I got a call that the time had come for me to settle the score with Vitale. He failed to find us in Milan but continued to look for my mother and me. He never gave up. If he knew who I was and where I was, he would snuff me out. The Sarnos said they had saved Vitale for me to erase before he erased me; just as the Davios must have told Rocco to either kill my father or they would have another Davio be his executioner. The Sarnos told me that Rocco was living in Manhattan, that he had medical problems and the name of his doctor. If I wasn't up to the task, they would take care of Vitale and stop protecting me and my mother. If I was up to the task, it would be a simple matter of self-defense. Vitale had already tried to erase me in Milan. He would have searched and searched had he not become sick. So, I moved to Manhattan and planned and waited to pull off the perfect undetectable crime."

Owen stopped and pivoted towards the Jury. Now he spoke directly to them.

"Yes, I killed Vitale in self-defense. If he knew who I was he would have killed me in an instant and claimed that he did so in self-defense. I'd like to think that the blast that killed my father was swift and painless, so I planned Vitale's death so it too would be swift and painless. I know what I did was against the Commandments that have guided my life's behavior, but what I did was also in accordance with the long standing CODE; the rules that I have been forced to survive by. THE CODE required that I kill Vitale. It was an imperative. Without the help of the

Sarnos, my mother and I would have been in our graves long ago. We are still at risk. There was no way, and there is no way, to extract ourselves from this mess."

Judge Tello dismissed the Jury; there was no reason for them to deliberate the innocence or guilt of Owen Holden. It was now his turn to deliberate on the sentence that he would impose on Owen Holden for committing murder. The deliberation would take several weeks and a prison sentence could be handed down with consideration of mitigating circumstances.

Chapter 25

Owen Holden was sentenced to a minimum of ten years at Sing Sing prison in Ossining, New York. Whenever Anna or John asked Shanahan to explain how he knew what they didn't know, how he concluded that Vitale had created the natural-gas explosion that destroyed Leo Lombard's home along with its occupants, how he obtained the secret Sorin Pacemaker memory print-out, and how he knew to inspect the fuse box and the door to Vitale's apartment that became so important in convicting Holden, Shanahan didn't answer. He asked them to be creative in their approach to obtaining clues. He told them to think like a detective and think like a criminal.

Several months after Holden's conviction, Shanahan scheduled a summary meeting of the case with Anna and John at headquarters. John had lost weight by diet and working out. He felt great and joked that he could have competed in the recent summer Olympics. Anna appeared to be stronger after her personal trainer had organized a progression of harder physical workouts.

"I'm here to finally answer your questions," said Shanahan.

Anna asked, "How did you know that Vitale killed Leo Lombard?"

Shanahan explained that everyone assumed that Vitale swallowed the combination to the safe and that it would have to be ripped out of the closet wall and blown open. He told Anna and John to learn to unlock doors and learn to be a safe cracker.

"Go to the scene of the crime. Immerse yourself in each detail; that's what I did before I directed you to Shaker Heights.

There were clues to Leo Lombard's death and other crimes in Vitale's safe. When the trial ended, all the unsavory contents were removed before Joseph Cornado took possession of the apartment."

"What about the Unique Sorin Pacemaker Memory Receiver print-out and Vitale's trip to Italy?" Anna persisted.

"Go to the source. Get your questions answered first hand. Doctor Peter Merlino got those answers from Doctor Joseph Higgins, the Sorin specialist. He also got a notarized statement and the memory printout that were entered as Exhibits A and B at the trial."

John asked, "What about the blown fuse and the door?"

Shanahan explained that the blown fuse shouldn't have been blown. It didn't make sense until the door came under suspicion.

"That happened because I had a mentor when I was at your stage. He told me to always keep a compass in my tool box. The needle that points north will waiver when passing near something made of iron, like pig iron or steel. There might be something hidden beneath the floor, above a ceiling or within a wall panel. The needle wavered when I was next to the wooden door. The door had to be carefully examined. It had to remain intact and be used as evidence. John, I thought you might catch on when I last sent you to Vitale's apartment to replace the Sorin Pacemaker stuff."

"I remember that the door was missing. I thought it was being exchanged for a new one. Now you're going to think I'm a dummy."

"John, don't worry about that. Now you know what I knew that you didn't know. Let's try to find out what Owen Holden knows that we don't know. Let's plan to visit him at Sing Sing."

The authorities at Sing Sing Prison gave Shanahan and Owen Holden permission to communicate by mail and phone as a prelude to their planned, brief, in-person meeting. Owen mentioned that the happiest and most formative period of his life was when he and his mother were together in Milan. Because of predetermined time constraints on all prison visitations, Owen mailed Shanahan a "memoir" of highlights during his six years in Milan when he was between twelve and eighteen years old. Shanahan shared the mailing with Anna and John.

All three of them were fascinated by Owen's long and complicated story.

> Upon arrival in 1962, Milan's culture was an incomprehensible puzzle for Mom and me. We were lucky to be greeted by members of the local church who helped us acclimate. With their help, we were able to find comfortable spacious accommodations. We didn't speak Italian. I was sent to a religious, church-affiliated school that instructed in English, Italian and Latin. My classmates were kind. They helped me with Italian and I helped them with English. My mother took private language and art lessons from a young woman named Grace Campo. Mother had artistic talent. She was more than a novice, having taken lessons as a youngster and art courses in college.

Milan was a huge metropolis compared to St. John, Minnesota. We had been transported to a place that had many industrial, educational, financial and religious institutions. Because of our ugly past with Leo Lombard's criminal, immoral and unethical behavior, mother favored our being associated with moral, just and ethical institutions and people that were not prone to ask many questions. Mother often wondered why Leo's brothers, Bart and Dom, told her that she must resettle in Milan. It is in the Lombard district of Italy. New arrivals to the USA who did not speak English were often given names that corresponded to their place of origin. Eventually, I surmised that Leo, Bart and Dom Lombard might have relatives or knew members of the Sarno Syndicate that would keep a watchful eye on us. We were ever alert and cautious about what not to reveal about ourselves, for we did not forget that we were the prey being sought by an unknown hunter. So we gravitated to the church. I was attending a church school and became a member of the choir. That's how I became an appreciator of liturgical music. Mother's heart was captured by any master's canvas of a biblical event that had her spirits transcend from earth towards the heavens. Another outlet for mother was doing all sorts of volunteer church work with Grace Campo. Italy was still recovering from the Second World War. Humanitarian projects were in place to feed the underfed, to collect clothing for the barely clothed and to find housing for the homeless.

Many of the museums in Milan had extraordinary fine art and the city was well known for the performing arts, especially opera at La Scala. Mother and I took tourist sight-seeing excursions. My school organized recreational camping, skiing and boating trips. As a member of our outstanding church choir, my horizons expanded when we were invited to perform in other cities in Italy, France and Switzerland. The religious art in Florence, Rome and Paris was an inspiration. The cathedrals made me believe that I would be welcomed in heaven—it was just a matter of time if I kept the faith. Each new experience made me happy and appreciative that I was being molded into a righteous young lad.

There were some moments of concern and fear. During several consecutive evenings a man arrived on a motor scooter, parked on the street opposite our apartment, and took photographs of our building. He lingered for several hours before riding off. Mother got so nervous, she rented a small apartment about a mile away. Several times each week I would meet her there in the evening where we would remain overnight. We never forgot why we fled to Italy. I imagined that tragedy might find us at any time. It never found us, but tragedy did find Grace Campo.

133

Grace and mother became close friends. Grace was very attractive, talented and marriageable—if the right guy came along. He did. Luke Messina was a handsome junior executive in the fashion industry. His ambition was to pursue the most sublime-appearing woman with universal appeal. Grace and Luke complimented or opposed each other in many ways. Her greatest talent was in art, his was in design. She was a humanitarian—a giver; he was a shrewd businessman—a taker who took advantage of competitors whenever possible. She was a devout Christian who participated in most rituals and celebrated the holidays; he was among the faithful but saw no reason to display his devotion to God. Most important was their mutual love which evolved into their engagement. There was a big party. Several months before the wedding date, the couple vacationed at the southern tip of Lake Como during July. The weather was excellent except for one day when a gale with exceptionally strong winds drove everyone indoors. Luke knew from experience that light winds during the calm after the storm would require a tall sail, so he rented a sailboat with a high metal mast. A stranger to the resort, Luke didn't know that a high-voltage electric power cable crossed the lake and that its lakeside tower had tilted during the gale. Sailors look about to avoid colliding with other boats or partially submerged fixed or drifting objects; sailors usually do not look up.

The weather was ideal for a day-sail about the lake. Luke was the captain and Grace handled the jib sheet according to his instructions. Grace had one hand on a sail line and the other on the side gunnel when the mast struck the sagging high-voltage cable. There was a spark. The boat tilted 45 degrees before it cleared the electric cable, but the tragic consequences had already occurred. High-voltage electricity traveled down the metal mast towards ground lake water. To get to ground, the boat was enveloped in the electrical field. Grace and Luke were thrown out of the boat. Luckily, they wore good life preservers that kept their heads above water. Passing motor boats plucked them out of the water. Grace's right arm, the one on the wet gunnel rail, was severely burned; it was actually charred to the bone and paralyzed. Luke was unconscious for several hours before he woke. With intact memory, he asked for Grace. He was not told about the extent of her injury, only that she had been transferred to a burn hospital. When he learned about the sagging cable and was told, "Both of you were electrocuted. You're lucky to be alive," he was furious that there had been no notice of the hazard.

Specialists in white coats examined Grace's charred arm. They concluded that the arteries, veins, microcirculation, muscles, and nerves had been destroyed below the elbow. The lower arm could not be saved. The upper arm had less damage and might be spared an amputation at the shoulder. Grace painted with her right hand. The prospect of no longer being able to display her God-given talent would have been daunting for most artists. Not so for Grace; she agreed to an elbow-level amputation. She knew that God would look after her, and guide her, with compassion. Unfortunately, Luke would do neither. In his eyes, Grace was damaged. She would never again have an ideal appearance. He called off the marriage and reclaimed the engagement ring. Grace recovered. She remained attractive and taught herself to paint with her left hand. She never dressed in the height of fashion, but always looked fine with a blouse or sweater sleeve pinned to her right shoulder. Grace enlisted my mother's help with activities she could not resume. One would be the Crown Jewel experience of my mother's journey in this life and the spiritual high point of my life.

The Santa Maria delle Grazie Church and Convent was located within a short walk of our spacious apartment. On an ancient inner wall of the Dominican convent is the original large fresco of *The Last Supper* by Leonardo da Vinci. It is the most well-known of all religious paintings. Leonardo lived in Milan for 19 years. His patron, Duke Ludovico Sforza, commissioned him to paint the thematic biblical story of Christ's last supper on the wall of the monastery dining hall. Duke Sforza was renovating the church and convent that was built upon the ruins of an old church that in turn was rumored to have been built upon ancient ruins that served as the gathering place of the Knights Templar —the warriors that did battle for the church during the Crusades. Leonardo took several years to complete the project. During the centuries that followed, the work has required frequent restorations. It was painted on a dry wall, not a canvas. Grace Campo was one of a limited number of people to view *The Last Supper* as she helped restore it with delicate applications of paint that preserved da Vinci's fine detail. After her tragic accident, Grace sponsored my mother to also help with the restoration. Imagine being in the figurative presence of Jesus and his twelve disciples. The building housed Dominicans, and the room with the painting was used as their dining hall. What inspiration and aspiration they must have had each day while dining and praying in clear view of Leonardo's masterpiece.

During World War Two, the Santa Maria site was aerial bombed. The roof was blown off and the painting exposed to the elements for several years. It's a miracle that it was not ruined beyond repair. Some believe that the spirits of the Knights Templar and the Lord above were responsible for that miracle. My mother's spirituality was overflowing while she helped restore the masterpiece. On one rare occasion she brought me to see it, to feel its majesty, in hopes that I would forever keep the faith. I honestly believed that I would. When I was at the convent in the presence of the Son of God, I believed that I would never be a sinner.

In *The Last Supper*, Leonardo depicted the moment that Jesus tells his disciples, that one among them is a traitor. He said, "One of you will betray me." When I was young and in the presence of the masterpiece, I truly believed that I would never be a sinner. Isn't it ironic that circumstances forced me to betray Rocco Vitale? If he didn't trust me, I wouldn't have been able to kill him.

Chapter 26

Arrangements were finally made. The detectives were given a private room to interview Owen Holden in the presence of a prison guard. Owen was as nonchalant and confident as he had been during his first interview as a "person of interest" at The Copley Plaza.

John was designated to lead the conversation.

"Are you angry at us for arresting you and providing the crucial information to the prosecution that led to you being here?"

"I'm not angry. You did your job. You're the good guys in a world of bad people and sinners. I had developed a perfect plan to eliminate Vitale before he could eliminate me. We were both trying to exercise our codified right of retribution. My perfect plan was foiled because you knew what I did not know."

"Can you tell us how you learned that Vitale murdered your father, Leo Lombard?"

"During the trial, I mentioned that it was a contact from the Sarno Syndicate. Why implicate others? I was on trial, no one else. In fact it was my uncles, Dom and Bart Lombard. They're the ones that told my mother and me how to evade danger; when to leave this country for Milan and when to change our names. They eventually told me where to find Vitale in New York. They told me about the door. The Sarno gang had it made after they tried to kill Vitale by bombing his apartment. They had a spy or two at his building and on the maintenance repair crew. After the new security measures were in place, the Sarnos couldn't enter Vitale's apartment through the removable door panel without being detected by the newly installed Seeing Eye. Over time, the Sarnos and Davios had each taken prisoners that were locked in their respective compounds. Under new leadership within each syndicate, they agreed on a two-year truce, a prisoner exchange and to void contracts on the lives of some enemy gang members unless there were new revelations that would demand retribution. Rocco Vitale was among those who had a reprieve. But he had committed so many ghoulish acts against the Sarnos, a new revelation might surface at any moment. Vitale was paranoid about being targeted, and for good reason.

My uncles knew it was Vitale because someone came to them hoping to get the reward that they posted. The reward seeker had information about Vitale being given a gas-utility vehicle from the motor pool. He paid big bucks to borrow the vehicle and keep the matter quiet. The informer came with solid proof that it was Vitale. My uncles never intended to pay the informer, because the reward was for information leading to the arrest of my father's murderer. My uncles had no intention of having Vitale arrested or convicted of murder. They intended to have Vitale executed by the hand of a Sarno or me. I wouldn't have done it unless my uncles assured me that the evidence against Vitale was solid. I trust them—they're family."

"During the trial you mentioned that your life would forever be in danger of retribution from the Davio gang. Do you still worry about that?" asked John.

"Not here. This place is no country club. There are a lot of tough guys here from the Sarno and Davio syndicates. They have a truce. No retributions here in the 'Big House.' I'm safer here than on the street."

Owen went on to tell the detectives that he was content at Sing Sing. He worked "full time" in the prison hospital. He helped the prison chaplain, Reverend Jeremiah, set up services and attended them every Sunday. Each day, Owen helped patients in the hospital. Some of the older inmates had pacemakers that he monitored for warning signs of defects or battery depletion. Owen said that he did not have a speck of remorse about killing Vitale and wouldn't ask a higher power for forgiveness.

"I made sure that Vitale had a quick and painless death. When I shut off the artificial pacemaker that was substituting its electrical stimuli for the total failure of his heart's own beat, Vitale just drifted off into a sleep state. When his heart's electricity stopped keeping the beat, Vitale's sight must have dimmed before becoming black. He might have heard voices of lost relatives, like his deceased wife and sons, parents and others. Then there might have been a bright light as his brain's electrical network failed. Next, a slight body tremor as his brain died. Finally, a peaceful death in bed. We live and die by electricity. I made sure that there was no pain, no trauma, no obvious weapon and no poison. I am a pacifist. In principle, I am a conscientious objector. No one should suffer as they die. I might land in Hell for killing Vitale. At least I planned and executed a swift and merciful murder."

Owen had told the detectives all he knew that they didn't know.

Shanahan thanked Owen for answering their questions and asked if he had any questions.

"I don't have a question, but I have an observation. I'm here because I lost and the State of New York won. In an actual historical sense, I won and New York lost."

"How's that?" asked Shanahan.

"Auburn State Prison in New York was the first place in the world that had a convict put to death by high-voltage electrical current. Sing Sing electrocuted the second, third, fourth and fifth on the same day, eleven months later. New York State believed the Hang Man had to be replaced because that procedure must be exacted perfectly for each prisoner. The weight of the prisoner, the thickness of the neck and the depth of drop after the trap-door's release had to be factored into the length of rope required to arrest the free-falling victim and neatly snap the neck to cut off sensation and air. Too little rope resulted in the Hang Man's noose cutting off air, a struggle by the suspended victim and death by asphyxiation. Too much rope led to a high-velocity decent that snapped the prisoner's neck, tore the attachment of muscles and tissues off the neck and could result in a gruesome beheading. Death by Electricity, or "electrocution," the popular term, was falsely promoted to be the answer to society's wish for a judicial death penalty that is compassionate, instantaneous and painless."

Anna interrupted, "When did all this happen?"

"William Kemmler was executed and believed dead on August 6, 1890, when a thousand volts passed through his body for seventeen seconds. Before he was pronounced, doctors found a pulse and slow respirations. So he was immediately electrocuted again, but this time for about ninety seconds. His death was not painless or instantaneous and neither were the majority of the next four here at Sing Sing."

When Owen paused, John mentioned that he knew of a recent decision by the United State Supreme Court that permits death by electricity because its jurors were persuaded that judicial executions in prisons with strict protocols were neither cruel nor unusual punishment.

"Maybe it isn't cruel or unusual if used properly," said Owen. "It's complicated. Too many times it doesn't work right. The prisoners are strapped down to prevent uncontrollable seizures; if they don't die promptly their flesh burns and sizzles and I'm told by the older doctors in our prison hospital that it's a horrible scene to witness. That's why I won by finding a painless and quick way to execute Vitale and the State of New York is a loser. They learned the errors of their ways and called a moratorium on executions about fourteen years ago. They messed up using high-voltage electricity; I succeeded by cutting off electricity. We live when electricity is properly respected and safely regulated, and we die when it's disrespected or poorly regulated."

Shanahan concluded the meeting by wishing Owen well.

On the way back to Manhattan, Shanahan briefed Anna and John about their next case.

STAFFORD I. COHEN

.

DISCLAIMER

STOP! GO NO FURTHER UNLESS YOU HAVE READ THE PRECEDING PAGES STARTING AT THE BEGINNING OF THE BOOK.

The author knows of no other instance where an implanted dedicated pacemaker device was purposefully shut off to kill a character in a story; nor does the author know of an actual instance where a pacemaker was purposefully shut off to kill a real person. In other words, the author has no knowledge of such a case in fact or fancy.

The first generation of pacemakers was not programmable. The second was programmable. *We Live and Die By Electricity* takes place at the earliest transition to the third generation of pacemakers—a generation that had a capacity to be interrogated; to print out pacer parameters. These prototype pacemakers had a memory that could reveal hazardous life-threatening or life-ending heart events. Rocco Vitale's prototype third-generation pacemaker was not marketed for many years because the algorithm that detects hazardous events was constantly being improved.

Owen Holden believed that he had committed the perfect undetectable murder. He would have succeeded, had not detective Shanahan pursued clues that escaped others, but not the broad sweep of his five senses.

The author asks: In the early days of pacemaker technology, were there any undetectable premeditated murders, and if so, how many were committed by evil technocrats that shut off a pacemaker? Murders that were overlooked and attributed to "death from natural causes?"

STAFFORD I. COHEN

Character Introduction by Chapter

Chapter 1:
Joseph "Rocco" Vitale—Davio Family manager and hit man. Lives at condo suite 1214.

Mike—Superintendent of condo building.

Joseph Cornado, Esq.—Emergency contact and defender of Joseph Vitale.

Chapter 2:
Dan Shanahan—Lead detective.

Anna—Junior detective. Daughter of a retired detective.

John—Junior detective. Son of a hardware-store owner.

Paul Pedonti—Joseph "Rocco" Vitale's primary doctor.

Chapter 3:
Hugh Appleton, Esq.—Colleague of Cornado.

Jean (Vitale)—Rocco's wife.

Chapter 4:
Jean Vitale—Rocco's wife (introduced in Chapter 3).

Joseph, Jr.—Rocco's older son, about 16 when kidnapped.

William—Rocco's younger son, about 14 when kidnapped.

Vinnie—Rocco's boss.

Father Bartholomew—Chaplain at Staten Island Hospital.

Chapter 5:
Paul Pedonti—Primary M.D. to Rocco Vitale (introduced in Chapter 2).

"Squint" Malone—Davio associate. Charged with a witness tampering.

Chapter 6:
Mortimer Baker, MD—Forensic Pathologist.
Peter Merlino—Electrophysiologist at Bellevue. Works with Mortimer Baker.

Chapter 7 :
Dan Shanahan—Lead detective on Vitale case (introduced in Chapter 2).
John Shanahan—Dan's father. A detective.
Terry Shanahan—Dan's mother. A school teacher.
Beatrice Shanahan—Dan's older sister. A nun.

Chapter 8:
Paul Pedonti—Rocco Vitali's MD (introduced in Chapters 2 and 5).
Mark Pedonti, MD—John's father.
Mary Pedonti—John's mother. A nurse.
Henry—Maitre d' at Grand Bella Restaurant.

Chapter 9:
Thomas Marks—Heart specialist and colleague of Paul Pedonti at Mercy Hospital.

Chapter 10:
Anna Dixon—Junior detective (introduced in Chapter 2). Anna's father is a disgraced detective.

Chapter 11:
Electricians—Speak about a Seeing Eye security camera with a seven-day back up, installed after an explosion at Vitale's twelfth-floor condo.
John Knight—Junior detective (introduced in Chapter 2).
Courtney Knight—John's father and owner of a hardware store.
Carrie Knight—John's mother.
Crusher—Security guard.
Bruno—Security guard.
Sister—Nickname for Frances, viewer of security cameras.

Chapter 12:
Andy Scarnici—Security guard.
Owen Holden—Pacemaker technician who works for cardiologist Thomas Marks (introduced in Chapter 9).

Chapter 14:
Peter Merlino—Pacemaker specialist (introduced in Chapter 6).
Dr. Joseph Higgins—Sorin Pacemaker implanter and consultant in Italy. Known to Dr. Merlino.

Chapter 15:
Helen Baker—Sister of Dr. Mortimer Baker.
Dr. Brownell—Neurologist attending Dr. Baker.

Chapter 16:
Leo Lombard—Blown up with home at Shaker heights, Ohio.
Margaret Lombard—Wife of Leo. Died in explosion.
Linda Lombard—Teenage daughter. Died in explosion.
Joyce Lombard—Teenage daughter. Died in explosion.

Chapter 19:
Bart Lombard—Leo's older brother.
Dom Lombard—Leo's younger brother.
Lucy Nardell Lombard—Leo's wife by bigamy.
Hugh Lombard—Lucy and Leo's son.
Dryden Pappas—Leo Lombard's lawyer.

Chapter 21:
Lou—Wounded demolition buddy of John Knight.

Chapter 23:
Salvador Verino—Prosecution lead attorney.
Ben Goldman—Defense lead attorney.
Anthony Tello—Trial judge.

Chapter 24:
Harrison Hadley—Industrial Engineer. Expert trial witness.

Chapter 25:
Grace Campo—Friend of Lucy Lombard in Milan.
Luke Messina—Engaged to marry Grace Campo.

Chapter 26:
Reverend Jeremiah—Chaplain at Sing-Sing Prison.

Stafford I. Cohen graduated from Brown University and pursued his medical training at Boston University School of Medicine. He has been a licensed physician for 51 years, working for most of his career as a cardiologist at a medical center in Boston. He has authored and co-authored many articles and research studies, published in peer-reviewed medical and scientific journals as well as newspapers and book chapters. His previous books are: *Paul Zoll, MD; The Pioneer Whose Discoveries Prevent Sudden Death* and *Doctor, Stay by Me.*

Dr. Cohen can be reached at:
staffordcohen@gmail.com

Made in United States
North Haven, CT
29 October 2021

10675146R10100